D1563018

the desert world

PIERRE JEAN JOUVE

the desert world

Translated by Lydia Davis

TᴹP

THE MARLBORO PRESS/NORTHWESTERN

EVANSTON, ILLINOIS

The Marlboro Press/Northwestern
Northwestern University Press
Evanston, Illinois 60208-4210

Originally published in French under the title *Le Monde
désert*. First published in 1927. Revised and edited version
published in 1960 by Mercure de France. Copyright ©
1960 by Mercure de France. English translation copyright
© 1996 by Lydia Davis. Published 1996 by The Marlboro
Press/Northwestern. All rights reserved.

Printed in the United States of America

ISBN 0-8101-6018-8

Library of Congress Cataloging-in-Publication Data

Jouve, Pierre Jean, 1887–
    [Monde désert. English]
    The desert world / Pierre Jean Jouve : translated by
Lydia Davis.
        p. cm.
    ISBN 0-8101-6018-8 (cloth : alk. paper)
    I. Davis, Lydia. II. Title.
PQ2619.O78M613 1996
843'.912—dc20   96-24732
                                                CIP

The paper used in this publication meets the minimum
requirements of the American National Standard for
Information Sciences—Permanence of Paper for Printed
Library Materials, ANSI Z39.48-1984.

In Memoriam J. L.
And for B. R. J.

FRIAR BERNARDINE: Thou has committed—
BARABAS: Fornication: but that was in another country,
And besides the wench is dead.

Christopher Marlowe, *The Jew of Malta*

Contents

PART ONE

Jacques

I

When the son of Pastor Isaac de Todi emerged from his chronic state of reverie to notice that the outside world, his father's "country place" in Geneva, was colored in one fashion or another by rain or by fair weather, depending on the season and the day, and above all on the unpredictable character of his own soul, he liked to descend the three shallow steps of the front stoop, out of the sad, solemn vestibule, then head across the great lawn, even if it was covered with snow, bypassing the "hall of chestnut trees," which exuded sadness, over the gently sloping lawn strewn with beeches, hornbeams, as though they had been tossed over the earth, finally cross the iron footbridge that lightly spanned the road to Cologny, and, after hurtling down several short flights of stairs, reach his domain.

This was the shore of the lake, pebbly and white. At this point it formed a natural harbor protected by a stone arm. At the end of the arm was a lantern where a green light might be lit at night; the light had a particularly true and sorrowful meaning on nights of north wind. The harbor could have contained a boat if Pastor de Todi had been less strict, and with that boat one would have gone off into the distance over the waves. There was neither grass nor moss nor dirt of any kind here, for the pastor's gardener was extraordinarily meticulous.

In this place one experienced a very great and pure silence, but if one thought about it, the silence was made up of noise, the innumerable sounds of waves collapsing gently. On the pier stood a pigeon house, built of the same gray stone and rising high above the water. For Jacques de Todi, nine years old and full of fantasies and mental stores, the pigeon house without pigeons on the edge of the lake took on the proportions, the aspect, the immense and accursed form of an Enchanted Castle on the sea, while the greenish tide advanced toward the meadows where sad sheep grazed, and the wonderfully changeable sky passed over the jagged mountains, and a terrible silence, a godly order, locked the castle, the sea, the trees within the same malediction, which included a small, negligible person sitting in a secluded spot on the grass, something like a woman. In fact, didn't Jacques de Todi know very well that this whole dream came from a painting he had seen? But no one could make him admit, when he was on the shore of the lake, that the painting of the Enchanted Castle was anything other than this, real and before his eyes: here are the mysterious waves, they surround the footing of the sad stone palace, solemn and full of the spirits of the dead (the pigeon house has no pigeons), the sheep who appear to be sleeping are no doubt on the other side of the road, one can see the mountains, and the small person sitting and trying to understand the meaning of so somber a story, even though he is feminine, is himself.

He would stay thus for a long time, until M. Delétraz, his tutor, appeared on the footbridge, called him stiffly.

It sometimes happened that he combined the daydream of the castle with another that was even stranger—a "true" dream, so to speak, as the person in the dream had been alive. Jacques would approach the water (during the summer, even on into the autumn); he would approach it, he would sit down on the pier, and the tips of his shoes would touch the waves. He would contemplate the water at length, passionately, plunging his gaze and his heart into it; he would become the water. He would experience, as things happening inside him, the thousand small torsions and green sinuosities, the eddies, the inner flows, the shivers, the lit transparencies, and the rapid passing of the schools of small black fish the size of a finger. When he had completely lost sight of all other reality (the blue skirt of the Jura opposite, the house—"Meadows"—near him, the image of his family, especially his father, Pastor de Todi, with his mustache and imperial and his profoundly sad air as he pronounced the benediction over lunch), there sometimes appeared in the water—that is to say, in Jacques's soul—an extraordinary figure, very beautiful and dreamy, as velvety as the water, not one of whose features remained fixed but changed and changed again. One day it had black hair, infinitely brilliant eyes with heavy lashes, a thin face, and brown skin; another day it was blond and truly gentle and pink like a woman; an instant later it assumed a tragic face with eyes and hair uncertain; or it even resembled his mother, who wore her hair carefully combed back and whose face was broad and pale. On the most precious, most beautiful evenings, the apparition was entirely without form, without a feature that one could discern or even imagine; it was without being, and Jacques de Todi extended his bewildered soul toward the living water in order to receive it, and gently, without using words, speak to it.

He was familiar with a photograph of a young woman dressed in the old style, with a piercing gaze and pretty face. He had been told: this is your Italian great-aunt; then, afterward, an impressive silence would always fall. Thus, every time the name of the Italian great-aunt was uttered, Jacques would feel a little shock. It seemed to him that a dim aureole would settle around the name, like a crown of affliction and love. Yet the person who had uttered the name inadvertently there in the parlor would quickly try to stop the aureole, without ever succeeding. What a name and what a creature! There was no relation between the creature in the photograph, that woman so astonishing because of the scandal she had caused, and the image in the water; no, no relation, but the image in the water was that woman herself, the magical essence of what she had been. If in the house of Pastor Isaac de Todi one did not speak of the Italian aunt except in a certain manner and with the greatest reserve, Jacques was not thereby offended, for he said to himself: my father is a man of God. But the Image, angel of another religion, creature of another world, became more marvelous because of the fact that a servant of the Lord could not recognize her, while a simple child of thirteen years, Jacques de Todi, recognized her entirely—loved her.

(Her name had been Paulina. She had lived in the Italy one sees in dreams at night. She had been a nun in a convent. In the end she killed a man she loved. That was eighteen years ago.)

Oh You whom I adore and who have come to me in the water, who have thus revealed yourself during so many evenings, or remain veiled in the depths, you are far more amazing, even, than that Italian aunt whom I love nevertheless because her life was extraordinary. The face contemplated Jacques through the water of the lake, covered with tears, and perhaps with smiles, Jacques being the only one in the world to know it existed, Jacques being the face, the soul, the eternity of the face and of the passionate love that so beautiful a face awoke. And the creature from whom this divine face originated had been exemplary: compared to the sufferings she had endured, the virtue of Pastor de Todi, even the goodness of Madame de Todi, obviously beautiful and holy, suddenly paled as though a sparkling genie had passed on the road and stared at the house.

Bella Tola

....

II

Splendid departure of Jacques de Todi, in perfect health, for Bella Tola at six o'clock on a winter morning, on his skis, almost naked.

Bella Tola is that dim triangle hanging in the dark sky like an odd sign. Complete darkness. Opposite, a long trail; a brown tide forms to cover the vault: day is readying. Stars swim noiselessly, parcels of pure, almost imperceptible rays, certain of them so intense they appear to crack. Another crack answers in the walls of the chalet where the pine is tormented by cold.

I am young. I am glorious. I'm off.

Of course the day will be splendid, cloudless, from half past seven on. The barometer was right. I have an hour of darkness for climbing. I can foresee everything. I swear that when the first ray alights on my skin (and my shadow will emerge from me, bizarre as smoke), it will be at that spot over there, exactly: the little mountain hut that lies two hundred meters beyond the larches.

Then there will be the pass; then the large pasture, climbing in Vs, a few rocks, it's done. I'm up on top at eleven o'clock. Not a minute to lose here in this dismal cold. So let's go!

I am Jacques de Todi, I'm twenty-five years old, I'm going around the chalet. The snow is excellent. Fell day before yesterday, froze, froze again, it'll be all right—powdered glass. Not worth the trouble to wax the skis. And even my long underwear—I'll get rid of it when I come down. Son of the Sun! And too bad, for God's sake, if I meet an Englishwoman.

Jacques's long, delicate, and rather hard face leans toward the

7

lantern that he is about to extinguish. His extremely light eyes—
too light—seem to have been washed by a torrent; his thin,
straight nose separates his face into two areas not entirely alike,
and his pale mustache imperfectly hides a weakness around the
mouth. As a person, he is on the whole good, dreamy, not well in
tune; athletic, he has a timidity that retains a clinging nature and
an element of Christian charity. I can say that I'm a strange
product. My father, Isaac de Todi, is the man who has the greatest influence over the Consistory and sustains the National Lib-
eral Church. No one has ever been able to resist his sweetness.
My mother was Italian and passionate, but despite that a good
Protestant (I still feel sorrow over her death). And I . . . ah, yes. I
am a "pure" Genevan. But . . . rebellious, and surrounded by
scandal ever since I turned seventeen! Free with a freedom I
bought, with a mind that I formed myself. In six months I escape
them for good to teach at the University of Basel. Of course,
Basel isn't very amusing either, but it's the door to the outside
for us folk from Geneva. What sinister people, what idiots, what
wet blankets! Their eyes are full of hollow dreams, their con-
sciences are "in good order," and everything that happens to
them is always good. Oh, their theology squeezes you like a nut-
cracker between grace and the virtues; but you can't do anything
about it, you're caught, it's the life of the Bible!

All my difficulties come from that.

All the obstacles to living, the false steps, the discomforts.
But I am healthy, by God, a "new man of the new life," and
without religion. I walk straight. I behave myself. I am in the
clear; I love, that's all. For instance, my friend Luc, who is a
poet, is always talking about my purity. No, not pure *yet*, my
dear Luc. Look at how my naked thigh bends when I brace my
ski to the left, then relaxes; that really gives me pleasure.

The man of the morning feels in harmony with all these
great crests visible all around, pierced with stars. Mountains!
Jacques de Todi loves you.

Jacques finally whistled in the direction of the window of the chalet where his friend Luc was supposed to appear. Luc showed himself, awake too early, enfolded by sleep and smoothing down his disorderly hair with his hand. Luc was ashamed to be so disheveled in front of the young athlete on his way to climb the mountain: he looked at Jacques with admiration and as though their friendship, a few months old, had suddenly been enriched by exceptional and precious values. All at once Luc swore: "But for God's sake! You're practically naked and it's fifteen degrees out!"—which Jacques answered with a few ardent cries that were muffled by the snowy atmosphere. And as Luc shouted again, "Take your sweater!" Jacques went off, in a straight line, all black, over the first little slope where the chalet stood, which led, with a rapid pleasure, to the most distant courses.

The fir trees, dark, inert, closed in again.

Jacques, embarked on the southeast flank of the mountain, must first leave behind the Lenz plateau and the forests; then he will pass for a short time over the west flank, then come back between the Wildstrubel and Bella Tola to receive the sun.

It's all quite easy, one is in fact strolling, really, over a great cone of snow. There's no reason to be tense. The pleasure isn't in the difficulty of the route: a girl could manage it. No, the pleasure is really in the hope of the sun, in the expectation of the sun that is going to come. Sun, dear Sun, holy Sun. Sun, still deceased behind the mountains, I am your child who is looking for you. I arrive before you. I have my eyes open despite the night; it is for you. I am naked in your honor.

(It's damned cold.)

My two blades of wood scarcely penetrate the gray surface, and yet if I turn around I see a trail, a sign: Jacques has passed. A confirmation of myself. It's beautiful. I'm very cold. God almighty I'm cold. I'm feeling what the first men felt, the great fear: the sun is about to be born. The sun will be born, the sun will be born. I, Jacques, believe in the sun. I don't know in what way, no, by virtue of what religion; it's all the same to me if it's a savage's belief or a scientific doctrine, but the sun is, for me, an essential generative being, the Central Energy which I worship, which I need, with which I burn to be united. Ah, I can make out the first ray, I sense it already, my skin is lighting up and my soul exists, the great cause is coming into play, the vital spirit, if you like (no, that doesn't mean anything)—well, anyway, the thing that for us has replaced God. Jacques no longer believes in "a God" (not his father's, not his Aunt Pauline's, not the Jehovah of the Temple or the Lord to whom one prays in secret). We, the new children of the caves, will be worshippers of the Sun. Over Jesus Christ, we prefer the totem of Fire. Alas! I am alone, I feel alone—the detachment is complete, the weakness is great. Be careful of the layers of ice, this must be an area of springs; the ski lifts and skids and one makes wrong moves. What was I saying? I was thinking about the religion of the sun. With suppleness, with equality of motion, everything is there, with cunning, with gaiety! I'm bitterly cold. But that's okay, *day will come.* The sort of brown sea in the background in which *it* is lying is becoming more and more brown, it is opening out, or it is rising, one can begin to distinguish the relief of the ground in front of one.

Jacques was very cold during this twilight before dawn; he was in the furrow of forests that kept him on the west slope.

He nearly turned around and went back down. Masses of fallen earth were not well covered by the snow. Fatigue. Tree trunks everywhere. Wrong steps and uncertainty. He believed that a large crystal of cold had settled on his chest and in the muscles of his thighs. (View of a guy exhausted on a very high mountain, who wants to sleep, who can't take any more, someone has tied him to his skis, stuck vertically into the snow: "Do you understand? You're to cry out *Ho!* every five minutes. We'll go and look for the cabin." Barely a quarter of an hour and nothing more, they listen, silence, nothing, the snow, the cold, the vise of the all-embracing cold. He doesn't shout anymore because he is sleeping, if he sleeps he is dead.) Come now, Jacques, calm down a little, my dear! Vision of the lake at Geneva on a summer morning: it's the bathing place of handsome young men, swimming, sun, swimming, the bodies are yellow or black, the sky is sure; one is safe, in the distance the bells of Saint Peter's are ringing, one sees the bodies of the young men, one feels love. (It's obvious; I left too early, and not wearing enough clothes.)

A woman's face with Nature's own hand painted
Hast thou, the master-mistress of my passion . . .

Enormous masses of sadness hide the sky. The day will never come. A star seems to sink, into what one doesn't know, and begins to shine again, and sinks once again. It is terribly cold. Fear overtakes you and there is no more celestial vault, that's why there won't be any day. Here there are larches, a few arollas. Standing in a concentrated atmosphere of melancholy, the trees are preventing the day from appearing. One feels the anguish of an invisible wicked presence. It is hard. Silence. Use all one's muscular strength to climb. And I have the ambition to be an artist, but I've done nothing yet, nothing; done absolutely nothing, I'm a nullity.

After twenty strides all that evaporates.

Jacques has turned, now he is in the east, he finds the open sky again. Well, it's getting on, it's progressing! One sees many fewer stars.

Bella Tola stands in the unblemished snow. In my life if only I could be as strong, as pure as it is. No more trace of tree or rock. The sky changes, the sky wavers, the light gathers. One sees two contradictory spirits in the vastness. Really day and night face to face: one russet and trembling; the other motionless, dark blue, like death. Three cheers for the day!

The day does not come.

The snow shows the characteristic bluish-pink tint; but nothing. Jacques is the god emerging from the sepulchre—nothing. Jacques takes enormous strides; he is frozen. The silent peaks appear, rise on the horizon, each in its designated place, and Jacques shouts their names: Weisshorn! Etothorn of Zinal! The Matterhorn hidden by the Dent Blanche, Monte Rosa clearly visible, the Mischabels! But what about the sun? Fire, energy? It does not appear. It will never appear. And yet the sky is clear, not a cloud. Jacques hears an immense moaning: it is in himself. I need the sun. I need the sun, the sun must arrive. More ardently than the sky, the snow, the forests below, and the whole of nature plead for the day; Jacques needs, has urgent need of, a ray of sun on his heart. He calls the sun, he entreats it. He counts the minutes that separate him from the sun. The watch on his wrist reads half past seven, it's time: what is it waiting for? This rotting light, in dirty diapers. Nothing, this isn't it, it isn't coming out. Jacques would like to say a prayer. I cannot find anything. What I know I know nothing about anymore, what I can do I can't do anymore. I need the sun. Give me the sun. This appeal to the sun that is going to warm Jacques's body takes on a character marked by anguish; at the same time it is beautiful, amazing, a delight. Jacques is at the extremity of his life; he totters, anticipating his imminent fall. He understands that he carries in his chest an enemy cold; if he dreams that this cold could cause him to die, it is with the pre-joy of a fabulous sun, and as the child of that sun, "for You . . . "

(That damned sun that won't ever come again—that deliberately turns away—the healing of illnesses—fear, my grandmother—I am stricken—Lazarus—my teeth are chattering—a weakling—organic defense—warm drink—to me to me!—safe, I am safe if the sun comes out—help—help—.)

12

It appears.

There is nothing now but the sun. "How frozen I am!" The ray reaches his skin, touches it; it is quite feeble. Oh, the ray burns, pierces, and I am saved. No, it has so little heat that one must believe in it to feel it.

An hour later Jacques is in the tranquil glory of rays and rays. A great blinding mystery is in everything. Jacques tries to understand the meaning of things and finds only rays, more rays, the substance of the rays, the warming of the rays.

III

Jacques was probably back by two o'clock. They saw him in the dining room and heard his loud whistle as he passed in front of Luc's bedroom.

As for Jacques's room, it was of yellow pine, on fire from the afternoon sun, and the flies thought it was summer there. Without any hesitation, Jacques collapsed on the sofa and immediately fell asleep. One scarcely understands what has happened when one awakes from such a sleep. An uneasiness was lodged in a distant place; Jacques breathed very hard to make it disappear. He smoked two cigarettes. He thought of Manuel. Manuel is a young Spaniard who lived in the chalet. The apparition of Manuel was so extraordinarily vivid that Jacques stood up: no, it was a fantasy of his brain. Then he developed the fantasy. Manuel as the Infante of Spain, his face pale, his eyes agate, is descending the dusty staircase in the courtyard of his palace. A phantasmagoric, erotic Spain, the color of saffron, pillions, mantillas, a spirit of grandeur and crucifix: for Manuel. I love you, Manuel, magnificent child. The Alp in the window disappears (with its evening shadows accumulated behind the pointed forests), then the Alp becomes real again: and I think he loves me.

13

Between one thing and another, Jacques thinks of Luc. They have been friends for five months. Luc is grave, with a flame in his dark eyes. Luc is clear, like a real Frenchman. He, too, is magnificent, but in a different way. The first time I met him. That day the cabin where Luc Pascal lived in Vermala was hidden, hemmed in, cut off from the world of the living by the most incredible snowfall they had had on those slopes in the last twenty years; the telegraph wires soldered by the flakes, the village gone, a single human figure at a window. And that eddying in the snow was someone, it was Jacques. They saw a great snowman shake himself on the balcony, go into a warm room.

"Luc Pascal?"

"That's me."

"Jacques de Todi, from Geneva." Ah, splendid, splendid, extremely splendid! I said to him: "I've read your books, etc."

Luc Pascal from Paris was a man already balding, rather dry: "I must confess to you that I don't place very much trust in friendship."

Jacques de Todi: "You will see, I swear to you we'll get along well."

Jacques rises with difficulty, he is hot and cold. What is going on in the twilit room? Here is the dawn sun: odd, pernicious, it casts forth its mechanical rays one by one in order to pierce Jacques's aching chest. A little time passes; someone knocks. Luc Pascal is there in front of Jacques, who is waking up, not having moved from the sofa onto which he first fell. "I don't know what's the matter with me, Luc, I don't feel well."

They go into Luc's study. On the table, like a dissected body, Luc's work is spread out in sheets of writing with many erasures and blots. He has certainly been working, no question about it.

Later in the evening, Jacques makes a new drawing for the portrait of Manuel. Young Manuel holds the pose with a naturalness in which there is a hint of insolence. He gazes cruelly at his painter. He is dressed in black velvet, which brings out the freshness of his slightly brown skin. One has the feeling that he is holding Jacques (but this is an illusion that the tall mountain boy allows to operate to his detriment because it amuses him). Even so, Luc is intrigued. Jacques, as he draws, likes to speak the childish language of the Spanish urchin: he apes his bad French; he has the rather babyish astonishment and naïveté of that young age. However, the child does not disarm; on the contrary, he attacks in a sustained way. Luc notices the change in Jacques's face: he stops joking and his dreamy features become hard; between the wrinkled forehead and the mouth whose lower lip is protruding his expression is tense. It's always like this when he draws, when he does a child's portrait. However that may be, the portrait takes form and becomes real: here is the sickly, sly, and graceful Spaniard.

IV

"This species of grimace on the part of the blackness and the whiteness produces the spectator. The spectator or the climber or the skier or the entertainer or the pursuer—in short, the spectator! This sort of serpent of a grimace of the spectator is more and more stifling. I have a dark gravity of a spectator in my chest. I have a chest of a spectator of pain, I have an obscurity of dark breath, the spectator doesn't like this pain, he doesn't like it. Dark tunnels appear through which the spectator passes. Mountains fall on the spectator more numerous than snowflakes or notes of music, and the spectator disappears, disappears with his blocked respiration, it's a story, let's not talk about it; he disappears in horror, in the tunnels of horror of the night darker than the dark night because it is made of darkness. Grimace. Leather. Hair. Grimace. Knee. Grimace. The spectator has entered the tunnel; let's not talk about it anymore, but the spectator is afraid, the spectator laughs, and his laugh uncouples the mountains whose grimaces are in fact the entrails of the spectator. Consequently the entrails, the intestines, grimace, and the spectator is crazy: *seriously ill*. Let's not move anymore! They're wrong about the spectator, he is entirely crushed, bashed, eliminated, his blood has come out of his body. The spectator will be interred. He was completely black and completely lost; he was a lost spectator because there was nothing to see; at a quarter to three in the morning in eternal time, the spectator had lost his way through the black fir trees but had found it again, and they have suffocated him in a room, and they keep him on a bed with his arms in a cross like the Lord, now the darkness that passes between him and his lung comes back out and goes down the road in the opposite direction with a bad odor! The spectator says, I am enclosed in abomination. In what horror he finds himself. For the spectator is not a man and is not a woman and is not a breath and is not a branch of a tree nor a naked leg on the snow nor a belly nor a buttock and not the least little ray of sun either; the spectator is accursed because he has heard the words *and that woman was covered by him*. Horror, slime, cunt. The spectator's Leviticus: *Thou shalt not lie with a man as one lies with a woman, it is an abomination*. But he doesn't care, he doesn't care, and hey, the spectator is sick, he's laughing! *Where and where? What is there? Pitch. Very sick.* Go away, o moral person! A piece of advice: begone. The spectator has only scorn for your attitude. He knows your tricks. 'Come closer, my boy.' We reveal what happens in hell where the spectator, deservedly condemned by his instincts, ordinarily lives. All his stories about blackness must lead him there, and the icy stream they put on his back changes nothing about that. Let's listen to the spectator. And you don't care about women, you say? Come here and take your clothes off, don't be afraid, I am an artist. You grasp the supreme wickedness, you hear it clearly: artist. The spectator in saying that trembles deeply, a manifestation of the obscure consummation of divine wishes in a wretched destiny, wretched! And you see him all prepared for infamy (you, Friendly Sir or Person appointed to care for the sick man). The spectator continuing: Adolescent, your chest is nice and flat and broad, you were surely born on the banks of the Nile and the sun varnished you with its kisses. What is he saying? What is he talking about? We can't hear and we don't want to hear! The spectator stands up to intervene: stop! But it is he, it is he, the hypocrite, it is he! Very odd these savage natures. The spectator does anything he likes. Perhaps, perhaps, my dear philanthropist. Still, there is something divine in it. Silence! The woman is a bag. Don't make me cry. Don't offend me. And at last! at last! the sun rises: what is more beautiful than my love and the sun, what is it? love! whereas the woman runs off with the moon. It's the sun that girds your loins and varnishes your chest and your heart; so long!—we're falling back into hell. The spectator permanently hardened in sin begins to purge his eternal affliction on the first day on the first day on the first day . . . and it's useless to approach him or even to try to form an idea of it or to love him or to care for him, useless, useless to approach him or even to try . . . "

V

The delirium had lasted from eleven o'clock until six in the morning. Luc staggered down the stairs. For seven hours, Jacques, with a temperature of 104°F and suffering from pneumonia, had told extraordinary stories shouting at the top of his voice—stories that no one should have heard and that not only had filled the pine bedroom lit by a nightlight but had even passed into the hallway.

Baladine came.

"Say, Monsieur Pascal," she said in her lisping voice, "I hear Jacques is sick?"

"Yes, he has pneumonia. Last night was very bad."

"Pneumonia. Oh. Can I see him?"

"No, he's sleeping now."

Baladine Nikolaievna is one of their friends; they see her in the afternoon or evening. They ski with her, dance with her. Beautiful woman. They don't know her last name. A Russian from Moscow, married, I think, to a German, but there has never been a husband. (This morning, because he is exhausted, Luc Pascal does not resist the intrusions of the outside world very well. He does not know what to do with this Russian woman, nor what she wants. Particularly, he can't imagine what her relationship with Jacques may be.)

In her person, Baladine is provocative. Once you notice certain movements her large body can make, you're no longer able to take your eyes off it. A fairly accurate qualifier would be "female bird." Long legs very pleasant to look at, arched feet, hips and bust present, but a gentle figure. I like tall women, says Luc. The broad, charming face of a cat, thin lips rouged, eyes ash-gray. As for her hair, it is provocative too, rather dark, sensual.

"Please excuse me. I'm very nervous. You know Jacques (I believe), he's a madman. The other day he went off before dawn completely naked; this is the result."

Baladine, more softly: "Is it serious? Come down with me, we'll talk."

"If you like. He's asleep and Manuel is with him."

Luc kept rubbing his hand across his forehead to erase memories. They went out through the hallway on tiptoe. Outside, a change of tone.

"So, you didn't sleep?" She looked at him with a cruel, almost laughing eye. "Why not?"

"He was delirious all night long. I'm still upset."

"Ah! What was he saying in his delirium?"

"Nothing, uh, nothing intelligible. A nightmare from fever,

you know, and from the night. Well, he mixed in with it a story about a spectator, I don't know: yes, he was talking the whole time about a spectator. They're giving him packings and injections of ether (because of the heart)."

Why does she want to know what he said in his delirium?

"He was talking about a spectator," says Baladine. "Poor thing, he is in distress. Take good care of him, I'll come back often. Good-bye Luc Pascal." (Distress quivers in her eyes.)

"Yes, come back often, Baladine Nikolaievna. I don't know why, I'm very anxious. Suppose I came out with you now?"

"No."

"And also, tell me: should I call his father?"

"It would be better not to." She added in English: "Please don't."

"Jacques doesn't like his family."

Luc's thoughts were elsewhere. Baladine's also.

What a beautiful woman!

"Good-bye. You must sleep, Luc Pascal. Sleep." She smiled with her dazzling teeth.

Once the Russian was gone, he was left with a knot of feelings to untangle. Difficult because of fatigue. Dancing shadows, like those on the walls of a room projected by the flame of a candle set down on the floor. And, really, I have never understood anything about Jacques. *Who* is Jacques? What precisely are the revelations of a delirium worth? Coherent fragments, incoherent fragments. Where does memory separate from hallucination? Yes, perhaps. That would be rather true. No. I need to sleep. And then all this has no importance, but only that he get well. All the same. I should know. Worry scatters us to the four winds. Let's think.

It's obvious, on the other hand, that this woman loves Jacques.

Didn't we often see her, last month, showing her pretty face at the downstairs window, pink from the cold, asking "where is he?" with a particular energy? If she loves him, it doesn't seem that her love goes much beyond fondness. The way she addresses another man; me for instance. Jacques's illness isn't making her frantic. She says, I'm going to see him and doesn't go; she leaves with a smile.

Could I be jealous?

(Jealous of this Baladine as a man, or jealous of Jacques as a friend?) It is fairly repugnant on my part to play at feeling desire for her; especially as before this morning I didn't concern myself about it.

Oh well, if I were jealous it would be of Jacques. I feel abandoned. On the contrary, isn't this woman looking so attractive just so that Jacques . . . ? But the delirium.

No longer to know accurately a man you know; no longer to be sure exactly who it is you love. You had a clear, complete image of a friend, you even made allowances for faults, for what is not very sure or very lovable in him. What freshness and goodness on the plus side of the balance! All of a sudden he makes a sign. (What do you mean, a sign? As he was delirious, it wasn't him!) You see a sign produced. A sign contrary to whom? To him, to himself, and emanating from him. Then he entirely changes form, is the same yet another. He reveals an amazing thing. How had he hidden it so easily? He hadn't even hidden it (Manuel). Even if he had confessed to it, no one would have believed it.

Jacques is indifferent to women, likes men.

(That the keen mind of the Russian should have grasped the secret right away was not surprising, but it added an almost intolerable pain.)

Second point. If Jacques is like this, it doesn't seem as though he finds joy and stability in it, and the particular circumstance is that he is looking for young boys. Is Jacques perhaps sick?

(Jacques de Todi, figure of perfect health, sensitive and not at all a neuropath, religious, tranquil, having the purity of the highlands.)

Third point. Why my aversion? His tendency and mine are inimical, what does that mean? Love in him and in me is equivalent. Love models instinct in its image. And despite everything, for my friendship it's a misfortune.

And I was therefore *only* his friend (the camaraderie of intelligence), and I have always given way before another friend whom he embraces, to whom he gives his life.

I am aggrieved.

VI

Jacques's convalescence was not so rapid. After many worries and discomforts, they saw the tall boy very weakened by his experience, "confined" within the walls of the chalet, then able to go outside a little, completely docile. Thus they forgot. A month later there was promise of spring, when the foehn begins to blow, relieving the meadows of the snow. The forests were turning blue, bits of dirty white were slowly melting, the warmth was coming, it was the time of thaw. Next, the flattened grass, buried for so long, stood up straight again in the air and grew.

If they were to leave this mountain where the season was rather arid, the friends would separate, Luc Pascal toward Paris and Jacques de Todi toward Basel. The friendship, reshaped, wracked by uneasiness, made them fear such an imminent separation. Let's stay until the beginning of summer, Pascal had said. During the first days just after the illness, he avoided Jacques; then the disturbance, the impediment he was feeling, had dissolved in a new atmosphere, he did not know how.

They had the idea of going down to Sierre for the festival of the Anniviars. The Anniviars, mountain-dwellers from across the valley, come down into the valley and work the vineyards there, men and women in costume digging trenches to the sound of a flute.

The valley, a steel gray or too strong a blue, has immense patches of rose. Departure. Luc, Jacques, and Germaine, Luc's girlfriend of the moment, are on a road that surrounds like a cable the meadows, orchards, wooden gates, and villages with their dark-brown houses. First they descend three hundred meters to discover spring: a gentle temperature, leaves turning green, streams piercing the earth without respect for the road and running over the feet of the walkers. The sky turns azure. Here are fruit trees. Jacques walks ahead. Luc says to Germaine, "How silent Jacques is."

"He's tired of his Russian friend."

"You're being silly," answers Luc irritably, "they're not seeing each other at all anymore."

"You think not?"

The water shines and creates blinding paths. The villages rise. They arrive, enter into them. The wind from below whistles in the distance. Soon the faces of the three young people are struck by eddies of plant smells, and the valley where everything is minuscule comes up to their belts.

"Spring is the creation of the world," says Luc (in order to say something). "It's been many years since I've sensed it the way I do today. Right, Jacques?"

Germaine answers, "This morning it's dizzying."

They encounter women of Valais dressed in velvet, under their hats like some sort of dead leaves, bony and beautiful, driving carts as they fix their iron gazes on a very remote spot.

"Beautiful, those women, wouldn't you say, Jacques?"

"They're all right."

"Amazing. Archaic."

"Yes."

"Is the walk too tiring?"

"No."

He does not want to talk.

22

"You already look better, you know? And you're moving right along."

"I'm twenty."

He has responded in a gloomy tone. They now smell the perfumes, the warmth of the lowlands. Everything is bright, distinct, resplendent. Jacques is dark.

Luc tries to understand Jacques's state of mind. Jacques, for his part, is thinking: This illness has put up barriers between me and everything else. Luc isn't the same anymore. He looks at me strangely, with fear and contempt, as though he were expecting something awful from me. I ought to get out of here tomorrow. I am the unfortunate one, always and again, the jackass, in fact. If I had stayed up there . . . Luc isn't the same anymore, he watches me. If I had stayed up there, I would have been able to take him into the meadows. Manuel, tell me what you have against me. Charming little thing. Why run away from me? I must have said something about it during my fever, but Luc is silent about that. He would certainly like it if nothing were changed. There, for example—why does he look at me fixedly as though he wanted to lock me up in order to hold onto me? No, I'm not going to fly off, believe me. And anyway, I'm Jacques, old man, you know, there's no one else—Jacques! Luc you're incredible. You get on my nerves, you give me goose bumps. I have to wait for the uneasiness to go away, I have to be good, be simple, and things will go better with Luc.

"Hey, Luc, tell me, what did I talk about when I was delirious?"

"Meaningless stuff, old man."

"But what sort of stuff?"

"Nothing at all. Nonsense, I tell you. Don't think about it anymore." Luc is already growing impatient. "Be happy, it's spring: *Heavens, gold, and winds, plains and mountains uncovered . . .*"

Everything I carry around inside me, Jacques's thoughts

resume, everything that is necessary, and the suffering, everything that marks me as a convict—do you know it so well, you who walk two steps in front of me and whom I call "my friend Luc"?

Noon comes. The road widens. Jacques would like to eliminate himself as the cause of everything he sees, of all the frightful feelings of this bright morning, because he is the source or the reflector of this dreadful sun on the valley colored by despair.

They don't know, they don't see. I am in the desert. The world is separating from me. Because of my sin. Yet that sin is my love, and my love is beautiful. The story is beginning again: I find friends, brothers, everything is good, I take hope, I'm hungry to work, I'm going to create my works; one day they learn about the thing, and they distance themselves. My strength. Because I seek the primary relationship among men differently from them. Because I don't *sense* what that means: Luc plus Germaine. But because I am not consenting either, because if I must live in my love, I find also my sin in it! Because. . . . Because I want all of existence, simple, honest, normal, me. Because I *also* need Luc as a companion (Luc has taken Germaine's arm), and if this Luc, while he is walking, touches his Germaine's breast, should I turn that into an accusation against him? Well, come on! God made me this way—no deliverance is possible. And however I may gripe, rebel, struggle, or submit, *I can't accept it.*

Cologny and the lake, the film of familiar images. The pastor turned in on himself and devoted to the spiritual life; Aunt Angèle de Todi always perfumed with lavender; tall Jacques . . . Supper in the evenings after the Bible reading, served by pretty Martine in her white apron with fluted flounces and her good smile. And at that very moment (they were entering Sierre), Luc Pascal, having received Jacques's thought telepathically,

24

sees Jacques once again on the lawn of "Meadows" telling him, on Christmas Day last winter, about an event from his childhood.

"Well, Luc, her name was Marguerite and she was my cousin. I was fifteen, she was twelve. You know, I was so in love with that girl it unbalanced me, as you will see: a real sickness. From love I stopped eating. I sacrificed to her my meals and my sleep. I didn't sleep, I stopped myself from sleeping, because I imagined that if I didn't unglue my thoughts from her for a single instant I would succeed in possessing her forever. She lived at 'The Elms' in Vandoeuvres, in that direction, six hundred meters from our wall. (Now, I really think she is dead, I've lost track of her.) I cut a class at least once a day to prowl around near Vandoeuvres. It was agreed between us, and you know, she was in it even deeper than I was. I spent half a day at a time behind a hedge, or under the porch of her farm, hiding out, or in the granary, or I would even lie among the artificial rock grottoes in her garden. She would bring me bread and chocolate and would slip letters to me: we were consumed by passion. If she couldn't come, I contented myself with seeing her from a distance; but then, in the evening, we would send each other eternal vows written on the pages of an herbal, below the plants, with circles indicating the places where we had put our mouths on the paper. One day we were like husband and wife in her bedroom, but you know, so nicely, I can't tell you.

"I was denounced, Luc, by 'The Righteous of Vandoeuvres,' an evangelical society for mutual surveillance. The family was summoned (except for my mother, who had just fallen ill), and then! Aunt Angèle, that holy spinster, was the fiercest, because she had received the denunciation; she therefore thought she was dishonored, and then even the word *love* would throw her into a state. In two days I was judged, locked up, sent away. The Pension des Roches in the Jura, with special treatment: no letters, no outside passes, no visits. The worst thing, you see, was that, instead of rebelling, I accepted everything as a punishment from Heaven: they had put doubt into my mind. I was guilty, see; I had to redeem myself. At that time I would cry the way you play sports. I became very religious. Marguerite had been bundled off to England; I knew nothing about it. This will seem funny to you; I never saw her again, there was always someone between us. I thought about her with shame, and to talk about her would have been an abomination. My father never alluded to the affair; that was proof that such a sin could not even appear as a memory in the conscience of a Christian. I became used to it; I was a profligate, and I redeemed myself as best I could. I was as sad as an animal, until the day I found my first friend, a gentle comrade, you know. . . . "

VII

They went to the home of Siemens the painter. Siemens was there. Siemens was waiting for the three friends in the corner of his meadow, in front of him the grass topped by flowering trees, behind him a background of mountains.

Siemens is a stout man in riding clothes, warm and tall, wearing on his head a lightweight cowboy hat, with a Roman face. (He lives in an old military tower tastefully converted. There he paints glacial scree, alpine huts, cows coming to water at sunset, soldiers with peasant girls in their Sunday best.) He's a friend of Jacques's. Introductions. Siemens, Germaine Marin. It is immediately obvious that Siemens finds Germaine to his liking. Siemens is a devourer of women.

Siemens urges the travelers toward his tower. "The walk down is superb, isn't it? And this is nice, coming from up there. Oh, up there the weather is filthy; in March, April, I refuse to go up. Whereas here, it's summer now, and what colors! It's a great time. Yes, I'm working a lot. So, Jacques?" The meadow itself is charming. "Your lungs, over and done with? But you're still a little thin, eh? melancholy?" (A great laugh.) "We'll take care of that. Lunch awaits you." Siemens's laugh seems to resound in a perpetual cave. These mountain men. Germaine Marin becomes very cheerful.

If Luc Pascal approaches someone else it is always with the feeling that between him and the other there will remain a small distance that can't be crossed and is for that very reason infinite.

He experienced an even greater difficulty in the presence of the artist type, for it is almost impossible for the principal in him and the principal in the other to correspond, or not be frankly opposed. But what could he do with a local artist like this one, belonging to a region of art with respect to which Luc doesn't even feel like an artist anymore. These green or violet mountains, these realistic rocks, this painting that tells stories. The painter's studio resembled a sort of church that had been perfumed with poetry—antiphonaries, old furniture, deer antlers, wedding dresses. Luc felt like the enemy of poetry: he would sincerely have enjoyed setting fire to the place. Where was his good humor of that morning, on the road? Impossible to extract a compliment from Luc, though one was certainly called for. Jacques, on the other hand, decidedly in a better mood, admired with enormous adjectives.

They take their places in the dining room—inlaid parquet and old wainscoting. A rather rich lunch is on the table (Luc has poor digestion). Good meal, dry wines, more or less general gaiety, Germaine very excited, talking about painting. Luc basically is interested only in himself, in the small circle of realities he has discovered and inventoried; this circle is too obscure and too thoroughly worked to contain what he has seen and heard here. It has been a long time since Luc has felt so enclosed and so crotchety; he makes all the more effort to disguise his state of mind. He succeeds, as Siemens shows a superb liveliness, and Jacques, tilting his head to one side, laughs with all his might. Germaine Marin has eyes only for Siemens; on the forehead of little Madame Siemens, a fresh girl from the valley, a pucker of jealousy appears. Luc, not being enough in love to defend his goods, surrenders his shop with the greatest possible politeness.

Strong sunlight on the high mountain ranges at three in the afternoon. The foehn was blowing, producing an intense sky and depths of a purplish-blue verging on black. They were coming back from the vineyards where they had watched the people of Valais working. Luc stood up from the low wall on which they were all sitting, below the painter's studio. "Let's think about getting back, Jacques. The funicular leaves at three fifty-two."

The sun was in its glory along the valley, which it directly faced. (Oh the tiresomeness of going back up there, and the fury against habit!) All three walked in the main street, Jacques first with his head bowed. They had seen the church coming, with its cemetery. Jacques was carrying Germaine's rucksack in his left hand, in his right dragging his cane over the sharp paving stones.

The gesture took only a second. Luc perceived the result before he understood the cause. The bag in which Germaine had stowed her things flew through the air over the cemetery wall. Thrown by Jacques. And the cane followed the bag. As Germaine cried out "oh!" Jacques started to run; he went terribly fast in the direction of the funicular and immediately turned left toward the Rhône.

A gust of wind carried off his hat, which remained on the ground.

"What's the matter with him? What's the matter with him?"

"Quick," said Luc. "You go get your bag from the cemetery." He ran off in his turn.

"I'm going to the Rhône."

"Yes," shouted Germaine.

Germaine in the cemetery: she found her bag, which was on a tomb. (Things broken inside.) Her irritation toward Jacques was not as intense as her emotion, her fear. Why not leave this bag, why not run? The sun filled the cemetery with a yellow atmosphere—simple, eternal. The sky was thick, like a blue liquor. No time to look, no time, and she did not leave the cemetery, she couldn't tear herself away from it.

The bank of the Rhône was miles away; she did not go there. She no longer dared go back to Siemens's house; she walked at random, and then there she was in front of the house. They were all there. Luc and Jacques. Jacques hardly recognizable. His face looked as though it had been rubbed with coal. Sweaty, shouting, gesticulating. He vociferated before Siemens while Luc squeezed his hand, pulled on his arm, also shouting very loud. Nothing could be understood. Jacques yelled: "I saw it! I saw it!"

What had he seen?

"I can't stand it anymore, I can't endure his ingratitude anymore! Listen, Siemens, I saw it: he made fun of you completely and thoroughly! Made fun of you. He laughed. You are good, you didn't understand. I care about the truth. I'm telling the truth! He was not respectful of you. I saw it, I tell you I saw it, I know his ways very well! I saw that he was making fun of you. You know how much he respects you? Not at all, and above all he despises your painting. I tell you he despises you! And also as a man. I will tell the truth in one word: he despises all of us." (Here Jacques, having freed himself, pointed his finger at Luc.) "He detests us. He despises us. Luc, you despise me. It seems surprising, what I'm saying, and it's exactly the way it is, Siemens, it was absolutely im-pos-sible for me to tolerate any longer a rudeness . . . to tolerate . . . to— to— to— to . . . A man as good, as brotherly as you, a comrade, wonderful, generous, I

29

mean, a host, I mean, who gives us happiness . . . happiness . . .
Well! the best things . . . the loveliness of his house! Not to be
thanked, but . . . ridiculed, I tell you! Ridiculed! You'll understand, you don't believe me, but you'll understand, when I tell
you everything! . . . Everything! . . . You'll understand . . .
Impossible to tolerate . . . "

Luc, trying to stop the flood:

"Jacques, you're crazy. Jacques, what you're saying is not
true and you know it. Jacques, you're sick. Be quiet."

"Monsieur Siemens, look at him, he's talking nonsense. No,
he can't defend himself! He can't even protest. Is he accusing
me of lying? Is he going to deny that he laughed in front of
your painting? Does he deny it? And he thinks you're worth-
less?"

It's rather painful to learn nasty things from the guests one
has treated well, admitted the plump face of the painter, and he
stared at Luc. The latter began to gesticulate as much as
Jacques, Germaine started to cry. But all at once Jacques de
Todi fell on his knees in front of Siemens:

"I want to prove that I atone before my friend Siemens for
the insults that through my fault have been paid to him. . . . "

Luc, his distress unbearable, left the room. Siemens and
Germaine lifted up Jacques, who was on the floor, sniffling,
and laid him down on a sofa. Siemens joined Luc in the garden:

"I knew him in the army, he wasn't at all like this, he didn't
have fits of hysteria. Look, what happened? . . . "

The day wasn't over. The five-fifteen funicular was carrying
all three of them up together. But Luc, observing Jacques's nervous glances, was expecting more outbursts. The shadows were
hastening to seize the mountain, moving in the same direction
as the train and more rapidly. There was to be a forty-five-
minute wait in the connecting station.

Jacques sprang out of the car with the same impulse to take flight that he had had by the cemetery. There was a race. He broke away easily without being able to disappear. At nightfall he was in the dense woods at the edge of the station. They shouted, "Ho!—Ho!"

Should they chase after him? Toward the left a large section of mountain had slid away; they would be driving him in that direction in the darkness. Besides, they were sure he was nearby; they could hear him; he was crying, a loud noise of sobs and gasping from a heaving chest.

Sometimes words: "I'm a wretch. I'm a piece of filth. I don't deserve to live. I want to die. I'm a wretch. I'm unspeakable. I dirty everything I touch. I shouldn't go on living. I'm a slanderer. I want to die. I'm a monster, a seducer and raper. I have fabricated lies against my friend Luc. I want to die. I'm unspeakable. I'm a wretch," etc.

For Luc it was a nightmare. The worst depths of Jacques having been revealed, the worst depths of Luc were appearing in their turn.

"Let's get out of here. Let's leave him."

"We can't," said Germaine. Against the sky, still tinged with green, the top of a little tree was swaying furiously.

"You see, there he is."

The little moaning tree was Jacques.

The noise stopped suddenly.

"Something bad has happened!" cried Luc, and he plunged ahead along with Germaine, searching the underbrush. "Where is he?"

A certain time went by, during which they heard the distant whipping of the foehn over the mountains.

The bushes opened out unexpectedly—the road leading from the village to the station. On the road, Jacques, and a form, a woman. Baladine Nikolaievna. Baladine's and Jacques's faces were touching. Nothing else, nothing was happening. Nothing, two statues. Two statues and a miracle (very obscure, like the meeting and the atmosphere). The force of two creatures, one of whom subdues, dominates, and restores the other. The struggle over, Jacques was defeated; or rather, the other Jacques was the victor, for he started walking submissively next to Baladine Nikolaievna, who threw back her strong, bare head, the head of a cat or tame panther, without touching anyone with a word.

VIII

In the weeks that followed many relationships changed. Jacques de Todi allowed the memories of his fit at Sierre to fall behind him. This was the good Jacques: his eyes washed by spring water; his honest, straightforward face. This time he was cured. Disappear, you phantoms, you clouds. Luc wondered if everything that had happened had any reality. He was inclined to consider the whole business the fantastic reflection of an illness.

The weather was fine.

Luc had quarreled with Germaine Marin almost right away, an outcome of earlier events unrelated to Jacques. At last he was enjoying solitude where his affections were concerned. He was "at work on his novel."

The two friends often met in Luc's room to talk about work, smoking cigarettes. Jacques was meticulously going over his thesis for the University of Basel. Parenthetically, young Manuel had left. Luc avoided noticing anything at all in Jacques's love life: wasn't this mainly because Jacques was spending time with Baladine?

The new interest centered upon Baladine Nikolaievna.

She would arrive with her wonderful abruptness. Like a gust of wind and always bareheaded, as on the evening of the funicular. She probably attributed a magical power to her head of hair. In fact, the sun remained imprisoned *in her beautiful burnished mane*, as Ronsard says.

Baladine would say hello to Luc, "Good luck to you" (in English), and go straight up to Jacques. The latter always welcomed her. He who used to call Baladine "an Asiatic plague."

What did they do? Jacques, sometimes on his bed or seated on the floor, was watched by Baladine. She smoked, he smoked. In one hour they uttered scarcely ten remarks. Jacques fled to the depths of himself, settled and fortified himself there. This woman was an angel of life whom he had to obey even though the angel formulated no command. One could hide nothing from the angel. To please her, Jacques had to remain calm and reflect. This angel made you happy. Nevertheless, a certain amount of aggression, bad will, and hardness had to find an outlet; and then a sly need to irritate her, to rub her the wrong way because she was so powerful. Finally, a strange pity. The emotion of people who have found one another in adversity. If one had opened the door unexpectedly, for instance, one would have seen Jacques on his knees before Baladine, who was painting her lips red.

It was an active companionship. Not a word of love.

Perhaps Baladine Nikolaievna was not indifferent to the color of Jacques's eyes. But Jacques did not dream about Baladine. He did not put his hand on Baladine's body, not even by chance. He was calm; he did not have an exclusive feeling for her; he only had a need for her presence, a regular, daily need, and once it was satisfied it left him joyful. Luc was no less calm with Baladine. Baladine read Luc's poems.

Baladine would tell them about little bits of her past, and now they knew that she was called Sergounine, had been married to one Reinhardt, and was presently getting a divorce. As Luc felt no agitation, he was not jealous of Jacques, especially as

Jacques probably did not love this woman; but Luc actually hoped that Jacques and the woman did love each other, he felt so much affection for Jacques.

Soon, and very rapidly, Baladine demolished Jacques's temporary home.

"You're nothing like a professor, you will never be Herr Privat-Docent. You should do paintings. You should paint. You're an artist, my dear."

"How do you know I'm an artist?" (He laughed awkwardly; he was flattered.)

"I saw you crying, *amico*, I know." (How casually she made her way into Jacques's innermost being.) "You must save those tears in a region that is *very elevated, superior!*" (She raised her eyebrows in a droll manner.) "I have known many artists. I know how they are; they are always naughty children. And I know the motion with which they cry. There are many ways of crying, but other men never cry like them, and it is when you see them cry that you can say truly what they are worth. You are an artist. Even if you paint badly for ten years, that is better than the University of Basel. For your heart."

She also said: "Leave your family, quarrel with your family. I want you to."

Jacques became noisily cheerful.

"Look how you arrange that, what an odd girl!"

Jacques left Geneva without notification, dropped philosophy, began to paint. And everywhere one felt the wing of hope.

IX

June morning—all the flowers, all the birds.

Jacques was walking in a little meadow enclosed by larches. He was treading through fragrant, delicious grass in which there were as many flowers as leaves. Above it rested the azure sky.

Warmth lightly spread everywhere, and wind.

Jacques was talking to himself. I know how to be happy like no one in the world. Clouds of worries, bad dreams—I turn my head and it's over. All I need is a summer morning. The sky. The earth. The wind. The smells. The soil. The light. Mountain, here's to you, mountain! You are the daughter of my heart, you are the object of my hand. Mountain, when one is on you and one listens to your motionless thought, one says yes to God. And then, what lights! Resin, hay, wild roses, and then what fragrances! The bells of the cows that are already grazing in the airy regions. I feel well. I feel good. The sky has my colors. I'm walking. I'm striding. I feel very well. The sun in my eyes, and the shadows. I'm even better. I'm better and better. In tune with everything that shines and breathes. Let's go into the woods. We look at the animals here. The fir trees are singing on the rocks, Siegfried's melody; here are mosses, pinecones, little branches, and the pleasure of snapping dead wood. Transparent green ceiling. Look, a big anthill asleep under its needles.

He entered a second small meadow. This one with a mountain hut, a red hut for hay. This reminds me of Bella Tola. But the difference, fortunately, is that Summer walks barefoot through the grass. Barefoot through the grass. A herdsman.

A boy watching the cows. He is barefoot.

A barefoot child.

He's a herdsman. About twelve years old. Tan and serious, gentle. Already of a somewhat Italian type. Well, no, that rough sweetness is from the mountains; it delights me.

He is whittling a stick. He is peeling the bark off the branch with his knife. He throws a stone at his cow because it has strayed off. He sits down again. He picks up his stick again.

Hello, child!

It's wonderful how fresh he is, a spring of water in a mossy vale. I think I'm going to like him. He has the goodness of the earth today. In nature the same as this mountain meadow above the last reach of the forest.

"Hello, sir."

The child has no mistrust of Jacques, and no interest in him either. There they are sitting close to the hut, which is old, tumbledown, all askew like a giver of bad advice (one can enter it through that little door with a latch).

"Tell me, is that hut yours?"

"No."

He has the taciturn character, the gentle indifference of people from these parts. He peels his stick quite as though Jacques did not exist. Yet Jacques is trembling, because the child's face is inscribing itself in him with more and more ardent strokes, warmer and warmer, more and more limpid. What grace he has! His clear complexion. The child opens charming lips, faintly swollen; above his eyes, a hard blue, his eyebrows are well formed, and an obstinate little forehead becomes lost under his brown hair. He is cleanly dressed in a jacket that has been washed often. The only poor detail: his naked, muddy feet.

"Where are you from?"

"Venthône."

"So far down. And you come all the way up to here?"

"For the cows."

"What's your name?"

"Stoebli."

"And your first name?"

"Charles."

The child steals a look at his questioner. And the latter shivers; through his whole body and even under his hair he shivers deliciously: it is joy. Because of Charles Stoebli, and because he, Jacques, says these words to him: "We'll be friends, shall we?"

The child indicates yes. Jacques has taken the two little hands in one of his and squeezes them hard. When Jacques relaxes, lets the hands go, Stoebli immediately picks up his stick again and carves.

They talk to each other for a long time. Tenderly.

Jacques no longer has any fear or doubt. Whatever happens, he is as happy as the sun. Whatever the danger may be, impatience and desire are curbed by a pure love that he avows in the presence of Nature. Because Nature shows him an endearing face.

If Jacques were paying more attention to his conscience, he would feel something being deeply torn apart (a certain calm, an acquired virtue), and he would see in his mind a sort of shipwreck taking place, that of an entirely contrary figure, red lips, blazing hair, who has followed him as far as this hut—only to disappear. Alone. At last. With him. The child. After the shipwreck, a great swirling within the deep, then everything recovers its equilibrium. Jacques experiences his nature. He is proud of it. The love he gives to the herdsman is certainly in harmony with the universe

These nymphs, I wish to perpetuate them . . .

but with a more extraordinary sweetness, more madness, and the magnificent sense of the forbidden. The child receives, like a secret he understands, a mysterious invitation. The desire and the gift tinge the mountains with crimson. These moist forests will be favorable to us. I touch his back between the shoulders, more delicious to my hand than the skin of a fruit. He is happy. Charles, you like the sun, do you like me? I lead him by the hand to the hut. He laughs.

X

Luc was working. Windows and doors opened to the fine weather on the mountain. The season made him happy. He was covering sheets of paper with his small handwriting.

The telephone rang. Siemens, from Sierre.

"Ah! How nice," said Luc.

"If you please, Monsieur Pascal, I'd like to talk to you this morning, at your place, about a serious matter."

"Come, I will be waiting for you. What . . . "

"No, not on the telephone. I will be up in an hour."

"Very good."

"You're the one I want to see, not Jacques."

"I understand. I will stay here and wait for you."

Luc went back to work. The ideas, the inventions, the sure phrase—all these turn around the pine tree, meander sliding over the sky, return to his hand, toy with the paper, and become a large page of black lines. Yet he is a little less than satisfied; there is a shadow.

At eleven o'clock Siemens arrives.

"Hello."

"Hello. Jacques isn't here?"

"No, but sit down. Will you have lunch with us?"

"I don't know, wait. I don't think so."

"What's the matter, my friend?"

Large Siemens is not at all calm.

Rather softly, "The day before yesterday, over by Lenz, Jacques encountered a scamp from Venthône, a kid named Stoebli."

"Ah." Luc's face changes.

"Last night I see the policeman from Sierre arrive at my house. I know him well, he's from my area, we were both born in Saint Luc. He thought it wise to notify me, seeing as I know Jacques, that a complaint has been lodged against him. By this boy Stoebli's father."

"A complaint. But why, what happened?"

"Regrettable things. Jacques used the child, who's a little rotter anyway and who, after offering no resistance, squealed about it all when he got home. The father is one of the drunks of Venthône. And verger at the church. The mother doesn't amount to much either. Stoebli hates outsiders. Yesterday morning at seven o'clock he was down there with his complaint. So it's no joke. If we don't stop it right away, the thing will go all the way to Bern. Very lucky you're here. But it won't be comfortable (and delicate because of the policeman). You'll see. Oh, I know them, my people of Valais."

Siemens looked annoyed.

"Jacques's a bloody idiot."

Siemens contemplated the scandal—affecting Jacques, Pastor de Todi, Geneva, Valais, all of them. "In Switzerland we don't joke." Siemens deplored the divulging of the facts, as though once the facts were known to the people of Valais they would change character. The facts in themselves were a matter for Jacques's conscience; and one could probably understand these very facts, actually, since one realized certain things. "For instance, in the army," Siemens said, "I saw a barracks room of eleven lieutenants, only two of whom had been with women."

And Luc? Entirely indifferent to sexual practices, that's what he wanted to be, without attraction or disgust or tolerance. Yet he felt a protest that certainly came from pained Friendship; thus, though he did not condemn the act, he did not accept Jacques's part in it, which amounted to the same thing; he did not tolerate this desire in the heart of his friend. The friendship also took note of the aggravating circumstance of *the child*. By introducing morality, the friendship deepened its wound. It was then that Luc changed roles and rebelled against his base manner of thinking: he discovered the need that guided Jacques. How could he doubt Jacques to the point of not relating this tendency of Jacques's to Jacques himself? How could he not admit that a part of the purity natural to Jacques had to be found preserved in the body of his act, and even in a certain sense (through the beauty of the abduction) illustrated by it? When one knew Jacques . . . Could a "good" man do something vile? And what should one say about the gift Jacques had given the child? How could one deny the gift—or appreciate it? Oh, what difficulties, what a cruel mystery!

Rumor having spread through the resort, the fashionable people turned their backs on Jacques. These people in silk sweaters distanced themselves with one and the same virtuous motion; and it was through them that Jacques found out what was happening to him.

Everyone—except for Baladine Nikolaievna Sergounine, who had a predilection for strolling around on Jacques's arm. Neither the fearful Jacques nor the confused or fugitive Jacques frightened her, nor the one with the weak smile who walked down the road blinking his eyes; for all those Jacques's needed Baladine precisely because nothing carnal bound them to this energetic and seductive woman. The disinterested Baladine had only to point out the path of life. On the other hand, Jacques under threat was afraid of Luc, his point of view as a man, his friendship, as of his logic, his terrible "judgment." He would take off as soon as a word, an allusion, reminded him that Luc and Siemens were struggling in Sierre to extricate him from a disgusting affair.

"Would he let himself be dragged into court and condemned? Would he stake his life on the outcome of this business? I don't ask him to help us, but at least to understand. No, he has no character. He reacts like a spoiled child." (They had intercepted a "message" that Jacques had sent to Venthône with the aim of seeing the Stoebli child again.)

It was Baladine who announced the good news to him three days later: "Everything is settled. We're compromising. You'll have to pay two hundred francs to his father."

Luc will always remember the scene.

The little room, filled with a group of men: the three men from Valais, plus the policeman close to the window, and Siemens chatting with the policeman. Jacques's room. The men from Valais are dressed up in clothes of a spongy black. The father is the typical sly sort you commonly see in processions between Brigue and Saint Maurice, the "underhanded" man who wears a full beard. He blows his nose often in a piece of blackish-brown cloth because his nose is full of tobacco. The wrinkles in his face are noticeable, as deep as dry ravines. The two others (his brother-in-law and a man from the village) are plainly nasty, ugly, and suspicious. The eyes of the three peasants turn toward the policeman: he is their guarantee, their support in an affair that is not ending as it ought to, according to the law, but that indisputably malign influences have directed otherwise; only the policeman can still grumble a little about the influences. For the peasants, the misdemeanor is obscure but all the more serious, and money is involved; Siemens is the enemy, he has the long arm. At this moment the mistrustful Stoebli remembers having been pushed against the wall by the painter: "Enough of this, you old crook, we'll give you two hundred francs and you'll withdraw your complaint. It's all finished, or else I'll make it my business to see that you suffer, understand!" The policeman is reassuring from the point of view of justice, but he gives no guarantee as to the sum of money. The policeman, sensing that he is being watched in that way, in turn places his faith in M. Siemens, known as an honorable man throughout the area. The policeman is in black and red, his tunic with skirts is of the Napoleon I model, his pants too tight for his belly, a baldric of white leather, buttons and saber. This comic-strip image does not smile and makes no audible noise; he is Swiss, he is duty itself.

They are waiting for Jacques. Jacques does not come. Luc would like to get the hell out of there.

The door opens. It's Jacques. This time the room is full. The door is closed again. Jacques remains standing against the door. Jacques's eyes seem canceled out; in his eyes the iris has the same color as the white.

Jacques looks for the father, to whom he *must* hand over what he is holding in his closed fist. He finds him almost right away, because the father shows himself. Is this old brute the father? (And little Charles his son?) The inanimate policeman lets things alone and watches; feelings are not in his province. In the presence of Charles's father, Jacques is suddenly dazzled by a truth; and human, sensitive as he knows how to be, he steps forward. He makes an effort to change in a single stroke his relations with this father, who is his fellow creature and Charles's father. The father is a man whom I have offended; then I will humiliate myself, I will ask his forgiveness. (Luc follows with horror this reasoning on the part of tall Jacques.) Jacques, what is more, is not reasoning; he is filled with Christian grace. With an expressive look, he holds out his right hand to the father.

The father keeps his hands in his pockets. The policeman gestures to Jacques to hand over the money. Then Jacques offers his left hand and between his fingertips the two hundred-franc bills.

"Look here, look here. Monsieur Siemens said so, yes, well, maybe so, but two hundred francs and it's all over and done with, and what about my boy's honor, eh? And what about my boy's honor? Look now, the law is on my side here, the law is with me. Look here."

Stoebli does not accept the bills but, raising his head and straightening his back, he calls his two stooges to witness.

Jacques turns paler. Now he seems made of wax. His grace leaves him. Luc is watching him. Inside, Jacques collapses. This is haggling, filth. Jacques's hand, the hand holding out the bills, trembles so much that the bills beat like the wings of a bird. Jacques does not try to hide his trembling. Jacques confesses his wretchedness with the tips of his fingers. Jacques abandons everything. But with his other hand he searches for his wallet . . .

Someone has to intervene, it's intolerable; Luc, Siemens too. Up to the policeman to speak.

"Because that was the understanding."

"Because that was the agreement."

"What agreement? If I was forced like that."

"Ah," said the policeman. "Well, that's different."

The thing is taking a bad turn. Jacques tries to find another hundred francs. Siemens plants himself between the man from Valais and the police officer.

"The out-of-court settlement was made with me, Siemens, concluded in my home, voluntarily on the part of both, I assume? People trust Siemens."

"Of course, Monsieur Siemens, naturally. Take the money, Stoebli."

"Take the money, Stoebli. It was understood that way."

"What way?"

"Two hundred francs. Take them. It's over and done with."

The policeman strikes his saber against the floor. The bills are taken and stuffed into a pocket. The three peasants put on their felt hats. Jacques does not move, he's a statue, a dishonored figure. The policeman is invited to have a drink of Fendant. They all go out. Jacques is in the middle of his room, Luc goes up and hugs him; Jacques does not respond.

XII

"I've been thinking about it. I remembered the night you were delirious and also what you told me about your childhood love.

43

Well, be what you are *by art as well as by nature,* as Shakespeare's line has it. Find a man like you who loves 'the same thing.' Give up the opposition that is exhausting you. Separate from morality and your family. Too bad for me, my dear Jacques."

"Impossible, my good man, impossible. And anyway, what I feel for you I'm keeping, and that's friendship."

"But one piece of advice, one order that we must give you: don't meddle with children anymore."

"If I were free."

"It's the price you have to pay for your salvation."

"But I want it, Luc, I want it! Honestly, Luc, I don't accept this thing. It is *in* me."

"What do you mean, in you?"

"It's someone else I know well, alien to me, and me at the same time, you understand? Who has a passion for this thing. He appears when it pleases him, or rather, no, he doesn't appear . . . I can't tell you what I like, if it's men or women, I have no idea."

"Someone else . . . Yes, the need, the necessity impels you, but you are responsible at each instant."

"I said someone else appears . . . then I corrected myself: I should say instead that I change. And it always comes after certain states of mind."

"What states?"

"For instance, when I am very happy in nature, when I feel that I'm in good health, when I want to be young, handsome."

"Never when you're nervous or melancholy?"

"Never."

"Well, then, you can see that clearly this love is connected to your strengths."

"No, it's a sin."

"Come now, do you still believe in sin?"

"It's a sin, I see it as a sin, I can't help it."

"And the other character, does he think it's a sin?"

"Well, naturally not. For him it's beautiful."

"Beautiful in the manner of ancient times."

"Yes, of course. Maybe. Or, then again, sometimes . . . He passes over it. He is strong."

"Well now, when you're in the midst of it, do you feel anxiety?"

"Amazing pleasure."

"I'm going back to what I said. If you have courage, and if you want to save yourself, you will create an equilibrium for yourself with what is natural to you, you will be a Platonist, otherwise . . . And anyway, what does all this matter: work—that's your reason for living. Love men if it helps you to work."

"No, because I will never be *that* . . . no use trying . . . well, let's not talk about it anymore, do you mind? I like a healthy life, Luc, old man, an honest life! I like the sun, humanity (you know, in the old sculptures from India, those giant women with breasts and bellies like globes of the world). I want to live. Hey, I'd like to sail off to Brazil or Africa. I'd like to know in detail all the life stories in the whole world! And in the end I am confident, you know, I am confident."

"Yes," said Luc mischievously, "and that's why you're tripping over one sin."

Jacques is in the train going along the valley.

It is close to evening.

The high walls of the arid mountains against the gray sky move scarcely at all while the train rolls along at their base: they do not want to let Jacques go.

Jacques cuts across and cuts across. The mountains begin again.

Good-bye for good. He has left. He has torn himself away from there, done and finished, gone. Already several hours separate him from the people up there, with fatiguing moves, waits, and the dust of train stations. F-I, fi—N-I-S-H-E-D—

nished. He packed his bag at two o'clock, suddenly, just after reading the letter from his father. He threw into the bag "the good and bad days," he closed it hastily, at four a last wave of the hand to Luc (the funicular is disappearing), at six the mountain was already far behind. In the station he helped the elderly porter by carrying his bag himself. He looked around him, saw only new people, and this soothed him. Opposite him in the train sat a new man. He talked to him. The man was a traveling salesman from Bern.

It's over with. Finished. He's free. Finished. Done. Behind him. He will never think about it again—his life up there and in Sierre. (Didn't even say good-bye to Siemens.) Done, the painful hour of good-byes before the departure of the funicular; it goes off, smoking over an ordinary mountain like forest fires when everything has burned. Yes, they suffered, naturally. But finished, delivered! Jacques pushes into the mountain crevices dirty things that happened, he hurls them down, he makes them die with a great crash.

At the end of the line Pastor de Todi is waiting. Basler Universität, etcetera. I don't think so. A catastrophe will take place, one doesn't know what. The idea of a catastrophe is restful. One can abandon oneself to a catastrophe, fall asleep over it, in it. I have no one now. I'm taking stock. My friendship with Luc Pascal is finished, I'd have to say. After what has happened to us, he'll draw up a general statement of accounts and find Jacques's assets to be zero. Baladine finished too. She was kind, but what did she want and what did Jacques want from her? Nothing at all. Germaine, Manuel, a rout of those people. General liquidation. Everyone will be relieved.

And Charles (the fleeting, sweet figure of Charles Stoebli). He puts him to one side. He still loves the child. Despite everything. Because of everything. This is the only thing that truly hurts him: he did not see him again.

Everyone will be relieved.

To what end?

Yes, to what end? They will forget Jacques. They are forgetting him already. Jacques is dying, he is dead. It's odd that the mountains do not want to move away, that they remain there; the train rolls along without stopping and yet does not reach Saint Maurice.

Oh God, what are you going to do with a man like me? (The sky darkens.) I'm curious to know. The storm, already seen, useless. The noise of the train replaces the soul, and it's only noise. Well, what are you going to do with a man like me?

He wakes up facing the lake at night. The mountains have disappeared but everything is dark. It is raining. At Villeneuve along the water, a great, black hole. It is Lake Geneva, abominable and necessary.

Here Jacques's heart turned over.

A soul, a ghost fluttering in all directions, flung itself upon him through the windows of the train. It approached, withdrew, confided a word to him. Jacques was afraid, he did not understand the word. He found the presence natural. Nothing surprised him. "Sin . . . " The interior-exterior voice was weary, spiritual. Am I making it up? Jacques de Todi said to himself. No, it is there. Obviously the same. The soul of the water. The soul still expressed regret for certain things difficult to grasp, through a discourse that gradually became voluble; but it seemed, as one heard it, that everything was explained, for what they necessarily had to have (it and Jacques) was a particular path, all the more beautiful the more wretched it was, the more ignominious. A womb opened. Jacques entered this wonderfully soft, eternal womb, and through the ghost of the Italian aunt of his childhood, Jacques wanted death.

Continuation and End

....

[BALADINE'S STORY]

I have to go back to the earliest period of my relationship with Jacques de Todi.

We were living in Geneva. In the new neighborhood that has been built down there on the edge of the Arve. You know it? The rue des Aubépines isn't a real street, more of a road along which they constructed four or five houses with many stories, and we were in one of them; it goes from the rue de Carouge, which is vulgar and working class, to a no-man's-land near the Cantonal Hospital. We lived in one of the new houses, on the fifth floor. This was in March 1911.

We had found each other again in Lausanne. There's no point in recounting how, it's very complicated. I couldn't live without him any longer, and I probably drew him to me with the force of my thoughts. He turned out to be affectionate toward me, and ardent in a certain way; yes, that's how it has to be said in order to allow our meeting to retain all its mystery. He was attracted by one thing in me, I was sure of it. We arrived in Geneva without a penny.

While he stayed hidden away in the Hôtel du Simplon near the station (he didn't yet have the strength to confront a new life, especially in Geneva), I looked for and rented this apartment in the rue des Aubépines. He entered it like a thief, but almost right away he felt reassured there. I decided to take an office job to support him and me. I found work at the Union du Crédit Suisse, 25 Corraterie. They paid me 350 francs a month.

I would go off every morning at ten minutes to nine. I would leave Jacques in his slippers in the dirty apartment. I had no choice, as that cleaning woman didn't come most of the time. I was *obliged* to leave, I was late. So I would look at him, my big Jacques, to give myself courage. In pajamas wide open at the top, which showed his chest, he would go from one room to the other. He was loafing. I knew he was going to sweep everything after I was gone.

Jacques was painting. His studio was the front room. At that time there was no doubt in my mind that he had to become an artist. My dream was to work on him so profoundly that I would make him into a great painter, something like Monet. It was very naive and stupid. I gave myself hope because I really had to. I love large things. And, you know, I know nothing about art, it's all the same to me.

Jacques drew and painted during the time he spent at the house—all day long, in the beginning of our life. So I felt proud in the evening. Before me, he had produced nothing, he was nothing; and now I had to throw his brushes on the floor so that he would pay attention to Baladine. But he had dropped the University of Basel and the rest. He had done everything I expected of him.

Imagine, he had said to his father in my presence: "I'm going to live with Baladine Nikolaievna here, beyond you and despite you, and we will get married or we will not get married, that's our business. I renounce in advance everything you could give me and everything you could keep from me." Yes, this was the hour of his great courage. It was a Sunday, I remember; the pastor was at our place. He's a sad man, authoritarian, who hides behind a false optimism, but that day he was trembling like a leaf when he looked at me.

"You are abandoning Christ, your father, and the path of honor in the very city where you were born."

"Yes, the path of honor! In this very city, absolutely."

Alas! Alas, my poor Jacques! One doesn't leave the Todis, one doesn't abandon Christ, one doesn't separate from such a father, I could see that.

The interlocutor now asks Baladine Nikolaievna, "But what object were you pursuing?"

What did I want? His strength and mine. Our salvation, if you understand me. I always wanted to believe that I was capable of greatness: there was greatness in linking myself with Jacques de Todi. Besides, I had faith in Jacques and I was in love. What was I seeking? Actually, I have no idea, no idea at all. Maybe I had found it good to purify myself with him because he was pure, or maybe to save him? After that I went on blindly.

Listen, what bothered me in my action was loving him so passionately. A simpler, more superficial love would have accomplished more. It often happened that I couldn't make a little salutary gesture for him, I was so immobilized, like a statue, by the violence of what I was feeling. Excessive desire, pity, and anger all yield the same negative result. Ah, I was no longer the Baladine I had been in Vermala! In Vermala I scarcely knew what I was doing, that was why things went so easily for me.

But the real problem was *his* love.

Now, even after so many years, I can't make up my mind about it. I have to say, first of all, this need contrary to me (me as a woman) that existed in him had to be acknowledged. I had known and seen this need during some hard times. I wasn't going to dispute it. There was no contempt, you know? No false agreement. I could fight with my weapons, but not pretend to be surprised or complain. If in that sense I had not been able to understand or accept anything, wouldn't I have had to let Jacques follow his destiny instead of summoning him to Lausanne? Everyone talks about these things, and no one senses what their secret is: jealousy is very different, depending on whether it is aroused by a sentiment of the nature of ours or, on the contrary, by a love whose nature is alien to us. Well, in the end I will say to you, the intuition I had of *our* life dissuaded me from mounting any opposition, for I knew that in order to succeed in my work, to live with him, to be loved, I had first and foremost to allow his tendency complete freedom during the whole time it might manifest itself.

So it was necessary to suffer enormously.

XV

I'm going back to when I left in the morning. So his day was for painting while mine was for invoices and numbers. The thought of it delighted me. In 1911 I had just been granted my divorce in Berlin; I was poor. My idea was that later we would have an adventurous life full of amusements, perhaps festive. It was good to begin with this purgatory and "numbers." After I rushed off like a gust of wind, he would restore order to the room by drawing the Persian silk cover over the bedclothes; he would drag the easel over to the window, because the light from the window was very inadequate in winter; and he would go on with his still life, or a landscape to be retouched, or me. I posed nude for him. Either Saturday and Sunday, or early in the morning during the summer, even before I washed. It often seemed to me that when I had just woken up, disheveled, with the smell of sleep on me, I had an effect on him.

His work was very difficult; the smallest thing would unsettle him and interrupt everything. And also the progress of his work was the sign indicating that our life was going well or not going well, for the slightest conflict, either from outside or between us, was evident to me in a canvas unfinished or spoiled.

No one came to the rue des Aubépines. We received no more letters. We had no friends. For the people in Geneva who had known Jacques, it was as though he were dead. The winter was very bad, very somber—but be happy, little Baladine: he is working.

As for my love for him, fortunately there are no words to describe it to you. I was infatuated. I was infatuated with an ideal beauty of his rather than with him himself; yet the whole of him was the cause of my greatest joys. I was pure for the first time in my life. My feeling went back to the day when I had met him on the Vermala road. He certainly did not know that during that winter I had spied on him behind the snowbanks, in the forest, and that I had been mad with anxiety when he was sick. On the other hand, he knew very well that if he went off naked the morning of Bella Tola, it was because, like a fool, I had bet him that he wouldn't dare do it.

At that time I dreamed of his great strength: I said to myself, one day he will take me away from the sterile life I'm leading. There, it had happened. And I would run to my bank thinking about it.

XVI

You don't know me very well yet, said Baladine to her interlocutor. What gave this love such value was precisely the fact that I am not a perverse woman, and yet a disorder exists in me. I will describe it to you: it's a state of dissatisfaction that in some sense lies dormant below everything I feel, and this emptiness, this desert, is summed up by the phrase "it doesn't matter," which I bring out involuntarily twenty times a day. I asked Jacques to take me away from the bad me. Thus I loved him as I abandoned myself, displaced myself from me onto him. I delighted in being his shadow, even as I took pride in leading him and loving him too much to pity him. And when I had been attached to his feet for a long time, he noticed me at last, and he thought, it's her. A very strange and fierce strength seized him, and he gave me my happiness.

Didn't I know that solitude was dangerous for him? One who so loved the life going on around him, the unexpected, chance encounters, so splendid when he was in the midst of tall fellows like himself! If in the course of his day he saw only a woman preoccupied at midday, with a headache in the evening. Was it enough to read to that woman in bed, to caress her hair before she fell asleep? Once night had come, he would walk out without going anywhere. Oh, how I would have scratched out the eyes of his last friends from the past, who not having enough heart to be with all kinds, now invented whatever little nastiness so as not to have any more to do with him. Wasn't it that ugly solitude which drove him back to the cafés he had frequented before, where he met all sorts of sports-minded boys with whom he mapped out races to run in the mountains?

There were still other bad times because of his impatience, my jealousy.

Before rushing off in the morning to the Union, I would swallow my too-hot cocoa in the kitchen, and as I'd burn my tongue I'd sit there disconsolately staring at the wall. You must understand me: I wasn't made to be on time. It was seven minutes to nine, five minutes to nine, two minutes to nine, and I needed ten minutes to make my way through the little streets, and Jacques knew that the head of the department allowed me five minutes' leeway, no more, after which he would report me to the management. This was why Jacques would grow impatient for my sake.

At first, I couldn't bear to be at fault in front of him. And the slightest sharp word on his part caused a crazy, ridiculous emotion in me. It was also painful for me to watch him making these remarks to me without any risk and entirely free of any restraints on his time, lying on the bed. For him—that is, for my love—I couldn't endure it. When he said to me, "You take a hundred times too long to powder your face," he was so aggressive that I had to remind myself: there is a much deeper reason why he's against me.

So that when I had suffered the other reproach from the department head, sitting at my place, I would begin, despite myself, to think black thoughts. Why did he try to drive me out of the house? (I knew very well that he had wanted to keep me from being late, but I went on.) Why always that scene? Couldn't he put up with my presence anymore—then why should I live with him one day longer? Or he was waiting for someone . . . (All of this in the midst of figures, interrupted by the telephone, and the typewriters making their wretched racket all around.) I think my jealousy at the bank was caused primarily by the fact that I was *at* the bank. So far away from our life, my imagination created monstrous images; I was too weak to drive them away, and in the end even the principles became false. What remained was a jealous woman, a nasty woman. I even went so far as to invent the idea that Jacques, wanting his freedom back, was pushing me in the direction of the head of the department—I should say that the department head tended to hover around me, and I had made the mistake of telling Jacques this to make him laugh. "But Jacques, listen! Aren't I forced to stay here?" And I would spend my morning in sorrowful invectives, in the tortures of love. I couldn't rescue myself until afternoon, when time took me gradually back to him. "I'm your friend anyway, Jacques, your true friend, better than a wife: for our love is great because it does not always exist, our love is a grace, we have to deserve it. I'm the one who makes you invent magnificent things! I'm the one who brings you back to me—not to a woman, *to me!* I'm the one who reconciles your life." This is what I told myself in the evening as I crossed the Bastions garden.

XVII

He would sometimes kiss the back of my neck as he passed behind me. But for weeks he was a chaste little boy in my bed. I was thirty-three years old. I think I was a beautiful woman. Sitting next to him (asleep, he was already dreaming), I tried to understand a puzzle, life was escaping me, or I would cry a little—and I only loved him the more for it.

When he was thus, without desire for me, I noticed that his feelings were good, clear, not at all violent or stormy. In this sense one couldn't imagine a more childlike, unfamiliar creature than he was during the first months of our life. Was love, then, really his sin, I wondered, for as soon as he recovered the temper of a man with that look he gave me as a woman, bizarre, irrational scenes exploded in which he seemed to me entirely changed. He said cruel things about me, my character, my physical appearance. "Your hips are too fat—you're powdered like a whore—your breasts show, and your nipples, you can't go to the office like that." At the same time, he needed to commit violent acts, throw things, break things. Clearly, I no longer had the power I had had the evening of the funicular.

When the nice weather arrived, he resumed going out a lot and formed friendships here and there that did not last very long. He asked me to welcome his friends to our house in the evenings. I agreed. Most of the time it was a fairly ordinary young man, rather nice and involved in the business world; he was exaggeratedly friendly to me. (Jacques fell in love quickly, praised his new friendship to the skies; and then it was over, we couldn't talk about it anymore. But when the next one arrived on the scene, I had to give my opinion, find him nice in this respect or that—in short, like him in my own way.) These relationships were begun on the Salève or in the little cafés on the waterfront. And if these relationships changed often, I wouldn't want you to think they were facile, superficial adventures: no, the event was always serious. Jacques always expected to meet the Unique Friend, the one chosen for the best part of his heart. He described to me what a life with three people would be like, based on the faithfulness of the friend and on his own (nothing could be based on my own faithfulness).

But I must talk about Taddeo Buonvicini.

Taddeo Buonvicini was a twenty-three-year-old from Ticino. A sculptor. He came more often than others, and he continued to come after he had been replaced. Imagine a . . . no, don't imagine, it couldn't be Taddeo. He was tall, pale, charming, and as simple as a meadow flower. His face turned to one side, beautiful features, a red scarf, very poor suits; large, hobnailed shoes that he dragged over sidewalks and into houses. It is true that he was as prone to blushing as a newly engaged girl and as secretive as a conspirator. He seduced you by means of a force that you didn't understand at all. And why did he remind me of Russia? Many times my eyes filled with tears because of him. He wasn't really a man or a woman; he was of a sex that one imagines in dreams.

I tried to find out who he was. No, which rascally ruses he had for evading my eyes. He lived at an enormous distance from all women (mistrust or indifference?), but without contempt. I thought of an angel; like an angel he lacked reality, and his tenderness was excessive and without any sweetness. Very energetic, like a young girl. Lunatic also, changing his desires, and even his appearance. He exerted a happy influence on Jacques: in sum, Jacques had found him, the Unique Friend; it was Taddeo, but Jacques did not know it and continued to run around.

When Taddeo succeeded so vividly in giving self-assurance to Jacques, whereas I had failed, I felt a twinge of jealousy; yet I liked Taddeo very much. Taddeo, who called me "the Sergounine," stole furtive, malicious glances at me. Once I had shed a few tears, it was over; we smiled.

The sculpture he made was strange and geometrical. I have told you I understood nothing about art. That isn't true. I felt that Taddeo had more talent than Jacques, and in his glassed-in attic on the boulevard des Philosophes I had seen statuettes that seemed charming to me, crouching or seated women. Taddeo knew many more things than Jacques, it was a delight to hear him talk. He taught me a great deal, he made me read; thanks to him, I was familiar with (for instance) Luc Pascal's new poetry. Jacques kept his distance. I thought about Jacques during my interminable days at the bank, and comparing him to Taddeo I understood that Jacques was still the son of Pastor de Todi. I had doubts about Jacques's vocation and the desire I had had. In that case, was painting a last resort, what one does as a lesser evil? He also worked less now, claimed he was catching up with "life," spent his time listening to the foolishness of a young cyclist or kidding around in the sun with a gang of swimmers. I thought I saw the truth: Jacques could not live, and for that reason he wanted to transport himself into art, but there he was afflicted with a weakness, a lack, and nothing remained but for him to fall back into a false life.

XVIII

We are into the second winter. Many difficulties. I was short of money. I had been upped to 450 francs because I was very bright, but I needed much more; we borrowed. At the office no one liked me, and the department head, once he knew about my relationship with Jacques, made my life miserable. I felt sad at that bank, very small, because my thoughts were elsewhere. I saw myself getting smaller.

Jacques was not doing well. When I came home I would find him collapsed on the sofa, impossible to get a word out of him. The worst days were going to return. Baladine, my little kitten, Baladine, you were mistaken, you were mistaken.

My anxiety also returned and I was attacked from both sides. I saw what our life was: a harsh desert country to be crossed, nothing but trees without greenery, black thorns, stones, a devilish sun. I walked bravely across this desert, but "I no longer believed in it"; I was exhausted not from having walked so much, but from feeling that the walking led nowhere.

Almost every evening a crisis. Nothing accomplished. Tubes of color on the floor and cigarette ashes everywhere. He had read books at random, had drunk some cognac, and when night came he entered into a predictable state of anguish. I switched off the lights and he moaned. If he answered my question— What's the matter?—he would say, "I'm feeling blue." No, he was no longer either violent or sarcastic. Oh Jacques, my crazy man, my treasure. But hadn't he already gone, leaving me this sick individual in his place? He never cried anymore as he had at Vermala: dry, wretched.

This is the game I was left with. I would go into the bathroom. I would put on a shapely silk dress in which he had done my portrait. I would make myself as lighthearted, as young as I could with powder and pencil. And, nervous, my dress on, my face arranged, my hair looking good in the mirror, I would utter softly the fateful words, Jacques, come back to yourself! and I would present myself in front of him. Sometimes he did not see me at all, but if he lifted his head he would see me. I would sit down near him. Without speaking I would allow my life to emerge from me like rays that I would send toward him. I was careful not to touch him. I felt that I was still powerful, but a prayer, the smallest prayer of a sinful woman before God—how much better that would have been! I saw him change, then inside myself I would worship him with joined hands, but I repeat, it probably wasn't him that I loved, it was God through him. And I saw him change. All of a sudden, he would laugh, Jacques would laugh. He would laugh, but that laugh—oh, it was the effect of grace! I, too, would laugh, more softly than he. All we knew how to do was laugh.

If Taddeo came a little later, the evening was saved. Then, tired, I thought only of sleeping. Jacques, lying on the sofa, smoked pipe after pipe. Taddeo would stand up and go over to the tea table. He would pick up the teapot in his large hand, fill the cups. He would bring mine, Jacques's, gliding lightly over his enormous shoes; he would offer sugar, lemon to Jacques, and milk to me. He was charming and very funny to see: the gracious young girl of the house.

XIX

We had celebrated our anniversary: two years. Don't smile, I was attached to these rituals. There were bad feelings, my depression, which was very painful to me. Jacques still playing the vagabond (I now felt repelled when he came back). I saw very clearly that I was growing mean. I was satisfied on the days when I once again found him lying in his sad state. I did not put on the dress anymore. I no longer wanted anything. Yet I did not relent, and then I celebrated our anniversary. But the misery resumed the next day, where it had left off the day before.

We were very unhappy.

The desert that extended within me to my very depths.

A desert without water, without strength, stiflingly hot, never a tear. No mitigations. However, let's see, my Baladine, what was new? What misfortune had occurred? Oh, the world could have a revolution or make war, everything could perish, nothing would ever change for me. It was evil. It would stay that way—imperfect, impure, unhappy, and always the same. I would not realize my great design. Jacques would be nothing more than Jacques. And I, too, the same, at that bank. I wouldn't save anything—of him or of me. And I would not even be just his woman.

At that moment your strength deserted you, says the interlocutor.

You know, despite everything, we were joined, as pain is to sorrow, and even in other ways, there was a glimmer of the earlier happiness.

Creatures who have suffered perfectly through each other know so many ways of being unhappy and so many ways of coming back in order to find each other again, it's indissoluble.

At the end of that winter of 1913, I knew very well that, deceived by him or loved falsely—who knows? soon lapsing myself? wait for the end of my story—I would never get free of him. And he? He would never get free of me. One settles into suffering, and one lives with it, unfortunately—it's terrible.

[END OF BALADINE'S FIRST STORY]

XX

When she returned, Baladine held out a letter she had received at the office, from Luc Pascal. A stranger. Luc Pascal announced that he would be coming to Geneva. He wrote, "My friends . . . "

"You know Luc Pascal, the writer?" Taddeo asked carelessly. Hadn't Baladine talked about Luc Pascal to Taddeo, and Taddeo to Jacques? Why these affectations of mystery? And Luc Pascal arrived in April.

Jacques had not written to Luc since his departure from Vermala. Baladine, on the other hand, must have written to him, because Luc was up-to-date on everything.

They were sincerely happy to see him again.

Luc Pascal first found Jacques de Todi alone in a little apartment in the rue des Aubépines; a more mature Jacques, stronger, more profound, it seemed. At noon his friend Baladine Nikolaievna arrived in a "cloud of melancholy," still attractive.

This cloud actually made her more beautiful, by softening her rather Tartar face. Her body, by God, was still splendid. In the evening, Luc made the acquaintance of a third person whom he did not much like, Taddeo Buonvicini.

And Luc was the naive and complicated man you knew before. With a certain added fame. Only a forehead even clearer and a quantity of little wrinkles around his eyes and mouth.

Aren't we still young, the three of us? said the gaze he rested on Baladine and on Jacques. Luc examined Jacques with the need to remember things well and the contrary desire to forget them. Baladine Nikolaievna welcomed Luc Pascal very simply. As for Jacques, he was in the full sunlight of happiness.

The conversation bore on three years. So you live here. Here is Jacques's painting. I like it. And Baladine's job at the Union du Crédit Suisse. Baladine. I like a woman who works, says Luc. Baladine shrugs her shoulders. Is this Luc Pascal an idiot? Readjustments, allusion is made to real pains and difficulties, to the general abandonment. Luc's faithful and persevering friendship, in contrast. "The reprobates of the rue des Aubépines thank you," declares Jacques.

Luc protests, "Let's not dramatize anything."

And again, "I believe you're very happy."

"Yes, very happy!" says Baladine ironically.

"I myself," Luc goes on, "have a hard life, work is impossible. *Anger is the state I am normally in.* I'm not happy in Paris. Paris is a gloomy, disgusting barracks. Far too many human beings. There, spirituality is as good as nonexistent."

"You probably think we're enjoying ourselves here in Geneva."

"Geneva? Magnificent. I'm on the Quai des Bergues, in a room where Amiel lived (they say). I can see Calvin's green city, the trees, Jean-Jacques, the sober blue-and-white waters, the frozen Savoie in the distance, a distinct and profound atmosphere, the most austere there is in Europe!"

Luc stops, impressed.

Well, now, when a Russian woman sets herself to laughing, doesn't she show a pretty death's-head.

XXI

Ease.

The early period is beautiful. The friendship is always new for being at all times experienced.

Jacques, as he looks at Luc, regains confidence. Jacques has always had only one friend, and he is this one. Jacques would not dare tell his and Baladine's story in all its details, as he would have to if the subject were broached; he is afraid of spoiling the friendship. It is better to convert into hope for the future everything that Luc gives us in the present moment.

Luc, through a bold conception, claims to find himself in the presence of an entirely renewed Jacques, Baladine's Jacques, and this conception in its turn exerts a salutary influence on everyone. As for Baladine, he does not really know her, but he divines the part she plays, and admires it. Luc in 1913 is alert, lively; his mind is clear, his body vigorous; he possesses the cutting phrase, it's stunning: relations with him are always a little difficult, all the more precious for that.

He is straightforward and visible through and through. He has no prejudices, no morality; what he likes and what he thinks he pursues passionately, one sees him darting between light and darkness. But the poet in Luc is something else again. You never perceive it. An admirable secret. Luc himself scarcely lives with it. As for the fashion of the times and success, this poet does not know what they mean. He keeps himself within a spider's web and stirs a little, the web being covered with all of nature's watery pearls.

Jacques examines his friend's virtues with the magnifying glass of zeal. He has read the latest poems written "to tunes of new logic," and he is madly enthusiastic. He buys Luc a copy of Dostoevsky's *The Idiot*, because they have talked about Myshkin together, and inscribes on the title page:

To Luc Pascal
Prime mover
from Jacques de Todi.
Geneva. Les Aubépines. 4. 5. 13.

In the evening they discuss things with fervor, with ardor and passion: books, men, society, experience. They lose themselves in the metaphysical sky, which is so close to us. Luc Pascal defends an art that pretends to join an angelic nature to reality, that aims to be the illumination of despair. Taddeo attributes supremacy to the beauty of forms and of number, and

Jacques opposes to Luc's ideal the immense suffering of humanity (for he is reading Tolstoy). Luc, to conclude, points to El Greco as one of the peaks. Baladine Nikolaievna is entranced by these strange concepts. She feels younger and watches Luc Pascal's lips when he talks. She admires him. Luc expresses to perfection what she, Baladine (she believes), would have wanted to obtain from Jacques in his painting.

When she comes back from the bank there is no longer a desert. The bank, too, becomes distant, with the monotonous cunning of the department head, the masses of invoices to be drawn up (business is good because of the Balkan wars). Life, outside of Luc, assumes a misty character.

During this same time Luc is writing his new novel: it will be savage, subtle, and as colorful as a movie poster. Because of this demanding work and because the restaurant is unsuitable, they decide that Luc will take dinner with his friends at the rue des Aubépines. Now they see him every day. They are told about everything. They witness his feelings of contentment when he has written the number of pages he intended, his excitements, his disappointments. They are present during certain depressions he has, and they support him. Warmth of spirit circulates among the friends, life is interesting, they truly have hope. Only Taddeo has remained the same—nonchalant, slightly perfidious—and because he is the same he becomes irritating; in the end, he drifts away.

XXII

Baladine's presence was acting like a shock upon Luc's heart: the effect of light followed by shadow, like a tumble into darkness. Pleasure mingled with distress. Soon Baladine's mane of hair assumed importance, and when she was far from his sight, he had the melancholy feeling that he had lost something.

Alone, he felt bitterness, along with a great incentive to work.

Baladine was traversed by a current of cheerful life as soon as Luc Pascal entered the room. The two magnetic movements occurred at the same time. It was simple and formidable.

In this area the terrain was completely mined in a few days. Things happened that they did not clearly distinguish because they did not want to, and others that they looked upon with complacency. The confidence that invites error and the tranquillity of heart that is not honest.

They fled one another by mutual agreement in order to meet each other at the designated spot. A few nighttime walks were devoted to serious conversations that had a clear primary meaning and a second meaning that was not formulated: "What exactly do you want?"

Baladine, returning at a quarter past seven, finding Luc Pascal lying on Jacques's sofa. (Jacques having gone out.) Baladine first thrusting away the thought of Jacques. Jacques is beginning to go out again. Then Baladine, doubly wounded and surprised, staring at Luc in her home engaged in waiting for her.

Luc reflecting—about this very beautiful woman, perfectly womanly, married (falsely); about the troubles that must form the basis of their conjugal life. It is true that Jacques did not recognize either homosexuality or marriage. Luc Pascal scorning his friend Jacques with the same impulse that made him love him, and scoring a point in his favor.

A little dark boat going off under the stars and marked by a single Venetian lantern. Jacques was rowing, looking at the heavens. Luc was smoking cigarettes. Baladine, in the stern, was holding the lines of the rudder.

Had he turned around, Jacques would have seen the lights of Cologny—and the spot where "Meadows" was (in the darkness). And even that green light that is not lit every day? That was, Jacques answered, the harbor belonging to the estate (and to childhood, religious discipline and tender feelings, dreams by the water's edge, the mystical friend, the image, Paulina Paulina Paulina). During this time, despite the darkness, Luc was seeking Baladine's eyes. He found them. He believed he had caught an animal. Then he lost them, the eyes having leapt away somewhere. He groped to seize them again, he sprang upon them; once they were seized, Baladine's eyes trembled, became resigned, allowed themselves to be covered. At Luc's first weakening, another leap, everything had to begin again.

XXIII

I'm not a nice guy. This is going to be very serious. What am I doing? I'm bringing about chaos. Sorry, I am just obeying, a very beautiful innocence is guiding us—to where fate wants us to go.

I'm an individual like all individuals, I get aroused by a woman.

So let's see. If I look at her hair, my head spins. If I catch her eyes with mine, I get pleasure from fighting it out with her. Her figure, her breasts, don't do anything for me. Her talk enchants me as though everything she said was breathtakingly wonderful and wise. Four different attitudes.

The fact is, it is remarkably stupid to have called "beautiful" a creature like that, as strong as a statue and with a soul that radiates a perverse brightness. . . .

She disturbs me, yes. She's got her claws in me. I'm capable of giving in, of going along with it. Of getting attached. Of getting lost in her. Yes.

The purity of the evening, what does the rest matter, the purity of the evening, Baladine and the purity of the evening.

Jacques—I don't care.

I think I'm beginning to love this Luc. It's terrible. I ought to leave right away. Not see him anymore. Luc my friend, I'm bad for you. But you drive me crazy, always catching my eyes like that. Go away. I love Jacques, and I'm Jacques's wife. How can you say. . . . You are pitiless. No Jacques, no my Jacques, you mustn't. I don't know anymore, it's pretty stupid. Surely there's a great danger. How did this come about? Already so far from shore. Could it be that he loves me?

"It's odd that in Vermala I understood nothing about her beauty, perceived nothing of her character."

"He is so different from the young man in Vermala, he is so much better."

He looks at me again and I have to respond to his gazes by making my eyes gleam. I know he likes it when my eyes gleam, so I respond to him. It's stronger than I am, here, take them; I give them.

Yes Luc, yes Baladine.

XXIV

In the twinkling of an eye Luc found a small villa in the village of Ongero. Ongero is on the border of Switzerland and Italy—lakes, mountains, stands of chestnut, cypresses. Ongero is blue. Ongero is blood red. The language spoken is Italian.

In the twinkling of an eye Baladine got from the bank her first real vacation, four weeks; she got it for Jacques, for herself, for Luc. When she arrived in Lugano, she was grasping in her hand, deep in her suit pocket, Luc's telegram: "Astonishing countryside, we shall be happy, come." She was going to see Luc dressed—how would he be dressed? It was very hot. Jacques in the post carriage seemed cheerful and swung his painting equipment to right and left. Ongero does indeed look out over Lake Lugano, across from Monte Generoso, that great, majestic machine of pure blue with counterforts (you distinguish seven of them) that quiver in the heat. The road is lofty, the travelers admire. Generoso is the "generous" mountain full of sweet promises, of Italy, of Veronese beauty—of happiness.

By way of a covered approach abutting the church, the carriage emerges onto Ongero's square: a sort of balcony upon the sky and backed against the pink-ochre facade of the *chiesa*, whose head is ornamented and curled. Luc in the middle of the square; he waves his arm, signals, "What did I tell you?" On the square before the church they form a triangle, and the suitcases, set down on the ground, cast very little shadow.

The house on the crest of the hill had a garden. Downstairs, Jacques and Baladine in two bedrooms. Upstairs, Luc's bedroom. A terrace here, a balcony there. They talked to each other starting in the early morning, wearing simple clothes; they touched each other at every moment of the day in the hallway, at the door, outside. The days were wonderful. They did not live inside four walls but in the heaven's air. They slept on the lawn during the first part of the night; in the morning they watched the sun explode as strong, as red, as the day before, and calmly expand in the green air. The light was a transport of space. All of a sudden it rained at midnight, with a multitude of lightning flashes, and the house, detached from the ground, went off like a stray in the thunder and water. Baladine was afraid, Jacques was asleep, Luc was pacing upstairs above her head. She would have liked him to come and sit on the foot of her bed. She was really too happy, or she was too full of sorrow.

The day after the storm Luc wanted to go down to town to buy some things Baladine would like. "I'll go with you!" she cried, but they gave it up almost immediately. In order to leave the garden he had to pass under a window: Baladine's. As Luc entered the passageway, he saw in the black window—Baladine.

Her eyes shining and her eyelids a little pink because she had been crying. Baladine, who is waiting for Luc. A single glance, going and coming, a single essence of a glance, and of love. Luc passes by.

They did not talk about it until the next day, among the chestnut trees as night was falling.

"Your glance yesterday."

"Well, yes, why not?"

"Can we go on?"

"I don't think so."

"So, I know your feelings. You know mine."

"Yes—so? What are we going to do?"

"I'll learn that from you."

"I'll never find the solution. You find it."

"You love me and I love you, Baladine."

"Yes, undoubtedly. Be quiet."

"I *think* I love you. It's wonderful."

"Yes. What I feel for you."

"Do you want our lives to be joined?"

"Yes, I want our lives to be joined. But how?"

"How you imagine it, Baladine. That is how it really will be."

"I didn't sleep last night because I was waiting for you to talk to me. Listen. Already, now, isn't it so, nothing can be the same anymore. I wanted to understand. Well, Luc, listen to me. You mustn't love me—"

"Too late, Baladine! The words have been said."

"—if we don't find within ourselves a secret, the secret of a life shared with Jacques, and Jacques must learn the secret too."

"Jacques."

"What is your answer?"

"I don't know what Jacques must be, or not be, or know, or what he will do, but I myself, here, can't take Jacques into account!"

"You have to, Luc, I'm Jacques's wife."

Luc gives a violent start in the obscurity. There is something spiteful he could say. The world becomes absolute darkness. Immediately afterward, Baladine gives her lips to Luc Pascal for the first time in the whole of life.

"All three of us must become one," she says. "I give myself to you."

XXV

Always, as though they wanted God to be able to gaze upon the greatest, the most fantastic landscapes, mingled with snow, or the most beautiful ones thanks to the succession and the super-imposition of screens of blue, they had advantageously placed those yellow churches with their poor magnificence and their slender campanili: in the woods or above the colorful villages, or forming knolls on the hills. He walked by himself. He loved Ongero. He left Baladine and Luc lying in the little meadow in front of the house, "since they are such good friends."

Jacques was healing his fear of life. He was emerging from a bloody nightmare, wisps of which were still passing in front of his sun. He would say, without understanding very well: I had a narrow escape. He walked, he rediscovered in his memory the walks he used to take, he stretched his legs and bent them again to feel the earth, he remembered more or less similar happy moments, he chewed on a blade of grass. The morning sur-rounded him with its grace and the evening beat down on him.

He was re-creating his existence.

I will marry Baladine. We have undergone the test and there will still be some bad days. I will marry her. An act of confidence. I believe in her. Does Baladine detest marriage as much as she says? Don't think so. Marriage is neither a spirit nor a sacrament, it's a symbol. Talk to her about it deliberately

71

and seriously, these days in Ongero. I will marry Baladine.

The rule of my new life? Asceticism.

I will transpose, deliver the erotic need, I will perform a miracle, fly away starting from here. No great life without a great mutilation. I will deny myself happiness; the boy walking by is my temptation, I am a tempted man, temptation will be the ferment of my spiritual life. I am silent and I love at the same time. I transport my whole heart into spirituality.

"I will learn to put myself in prison." A more distant echo behind a mountain answered, "You must seek God."

Jacques was walking with great, calm strides; he had a mad hope. His shirt open over his torso down to his belt, his pants laced up with a leather thong, a panama hat pushed down over his eyes and covering his nape—this was a man passing through nature or a mystic passing beyond it. Every thought and every motion abolished, empty, suspended, he went on despite the heat, climbing, descending; he would never stop.

As he was passing through the midst of the underbrush that exhales warm air at nightfall, he recalled more distant, more personal experiences. "I am acquainted with everything, I know all that." He looked vaguely toward Generoso; behind it was Lake Como. I have never seen it. An apparition: he is at the edge of the water and toward him comes Aunt Paulina, who is strolling around under the black cypresses, arm in arm with her lover. Jacques holds his breath, shivers with fear, with pleasure. Death is passing say the old people.

XXVI

He came back trembling with fatigue and found them lying on the grass, Baladine very visible in a white dress; it was as though they had not moved all day.

"Good evening!"

"Good evening, Jacques." (He or she spoke with an effort.)

"What have you two been doing?"

"Nothing. Not much."

Night and the stars. Happy, mysterious, Jacques lay down next to his friends; then a vast silence began.

During all the hours that tall Jacques was walking, Luc had indeed remained next to Baladine, tight against her, pressing her to give in to him, having only one idea: to conquer her. He surrounded her with his murmuring, but he lacked the rude strength that would have ended the struggle. Luc was allowed to kiss Baladine's dry lips, with more difficulty her half-open mouth; but her tongue, with its intimate consent, was still denied him.

Baladine, tired and dazed, who had defended herself so well, remained under the charm and meditated on the terrible love. Baladine, the object of a physical love and at the same time of a sacred magic appeal, which made him unable to desire anything other than identification with her, through raw penetration into her body. The act is necessary; nothing will be true any longer before the act, his painful life hangs upon the act; but after the act infinite perspectives will reveal themselves.

Jacques, always Jacques.

"Leave him, I will marry you."

"No, never; we haven't found anything yet."

She said also: "And you know, I will be a disappointment to you. You will learn that immediately after you have loved me."

Leave me alone, go within the hour! What does it matter anyway? Life is over. Turn your eyes toward me again, turn them like that, I adore you.

"Leave for Paris, will you?"

Not tomorrow, that would be too late, this evening, no . . .

this very moment. Leave without saying good-bye to me. Maybe I will die, but I love you too much to endure having you here one day longer. . . . But you know, I will certainly not die. Luc, I love you so much!

"Leave! No, stay."

Nothing would be accomplished at Ongero, they felt that now, everything would be done elsewhere.

Baladine's abandon increased. Abysses opened sweetly. Their faces changed—suffering, concupiscence. Did Jacques begin to perceive a disturbance surrounding his two friends and in his house? Jacques, who said to Baladine in the first days, "You are happier at Ongero than I have ever seen you before." And now: "You seem distracted, you're strange, are you having a bad time? Let's go back to Geneva. If you walked outside with me, I would tell you things; I myself am terribly fond of the country, you know." Baladine refused three times in succession and gave in the fourth. A disaster: the walk was dismal because Jacques perceived in Baladine such distress that not one of his hopes was left to him, and his mouth could not emit a word. Even though the sun was yellow and the sky deep under the chestnuts and the air, packed with luminous insects, was traversed by the most beautiful butterflies, they said nothing. (And if they could have seen Luc—he was pacing around in the cage of the house like a madman.) Jacques imagined that Luc was having a fit of nastiness and "setting" Baladine against him. Luc was no longer the same, Luc resented him; quantities of signs strengthened him in that opinion.

In fact, Luc was scything flowers and mutilating trees in order to exhaust his anger and not leap at Jacques's throat when he saw him again "with his woman." Luc obsessed by the image of Baladine's breast glimpsed that morning near the bathroom; Luc seeing Jacques lying on the ground dead; Luc turning his back on that blue-tinged nature; Luc, who hated Ongero, went out onto the lawn to kiss the spot where the grass had been crushed by Baladine's body.

"I reject the impure suggestions of a life shared by three: (1) I sleep with Baladine; (2) I quarrel with Jacques; (3) I take Baladine away."

XXVII

Jacques, taciturn, starting at dawn, goes off over Erbea Hill; he stays the night there, too. One day they see him pass by with a dirty little boy from the village.

Luc is sleepless, but he holds his own. He will have what he wants. Soon. He will have it with full consent and not as a seduction. Once again life gives Luc an occasion to look down upon Jacques.

Baladine is more and more humble. This is not Baladine; she no longer has any influence over anyone. She's a girl in a woolen dress who displays herself for Luc and whom we see walking, aimed at like a target. Or she is seated in front of her suicide, which she looks at with pleasure, or even, more simply as a door that someone is going to open. It's stupid.

The departure comes quickly. Ongero no longer wants these three ill-starred travelers.

Baladine can still observe from a distance what Jacques is doing: he resembles a swallow skimming the earth before a storm. He is frightful, in what way no one knows. I know him so well (and Baladine sheds a tear).

It's time to leave.

Luc has made the decision. Jacques has answered yes as though he were saying, "I was expecting this." One splendid morning they leave Ongero without looking back. During the descent in the carriage, Baladine cannot take her eyes off

Jacques's face (his pale eyes). He knows, he knows, he has understood. But Jacques points his finger at the lines of smiling villages on the edge of the water that they are seeing for the last time.

Baladine now has only one force in her: Luc Pascal exists.

They spend the night in Lucerne. They have been given three rooms on different floors. Jacques has gone to sleep. Luc and Baladine take each other at three o'clock in the morning, in Luc's room.

What Jacques had felt in the train through the Gothard was a collapse, a bankruptcy, an end. Nothing left of what had been experienced and dreamed, and, I find myself in front of a wall.

They will sleep together tonight—I suppose.

He suffered too much: no more pain. Nerves on edge. Only a vague feeling of something irreparable and of the fate that is in motion from now on.

He was occupied with breathing. He counted the motions for expanding his chest: one, two, three, four, up to a hundred. He said to himself, as though his life depended on it, breathe up to five thousand.

One knows very well that one can't live.

One knows very well. . . . One knows very well that death is unintelligible. Well.

Secretly he took Luc's face, joined it to Baladine's opposite him: the greatest sin that God must punish is betrayal. They saw nothing, they thought about each other. They made a show of being cheerful, a railway car cheerfulness. Very well! Jacques would set to work at being cheerful too! But he did not have time, for in one of the twisting tunnels his ears buzzed, he lost consciousness. The daylight revived him. His friends had disappeared.

Where were they? In the restaurant car or elsewhere? Jacques left the compartment and stood at an open window. Alone in the rush of air; and the wind dried his tears.

At Lucerne he fell on his bed, overcome by sleep. But at Geneva, the next day, it was a sleepwalker who disembarked next to a tragic woman (the man Luc, having remained behind, would follow by the next train). I must do something, he said to himself, must do something, do something. The light in the streets insulted him. He wanted to spit on what shone and bury his head in a cellar in order to think.

At home, Jacques left the blinds closed, went to bed fully clothed, his eyes on the ceiling. To be comfortable, he should also have closed his eyes, closed them, but it was no use. Baladine went back out almost right away.

XXVIII

[BALADINE'S SECOND STORY]

Allow me not to talk about it. These are things of life inexplicable to the person who has experienced them, so I will be silent. But you know what happened at Ongero and after. I also will not talk about pangs and remorse. That's useless. Thus it's quite possible I will appear to you unpleasant, dry, hard, and it is strange that I must appear that way to you.

A whole part of my life is closed, buried as though in a crypt. Never again will I look at what still exists as memory in that spot. Only in this way can I live and tell you what came next. The things in my heart for Jacques are what must be told.

These events occurred between August and November; not much time, you see. Don't ask me questions. You have to let me talk peacefully, I must be able to let myself go, that's how you will find out the truth.

A few words: my love for Luc Pascal at Lucerne gave me the greatest desire to die that I've ever had. If I did not do away with myself the next morning, it was undoubtedly because a chambermaid prevented me by her presence. What had happened was the work of the devil. We can become devils ourselves, isn't that so? A man and a woman who possess each other in a hotel, keeping watch on a door that could open and searching for all the ways of obtaining the greatest possible pleasure, when both of them have, inside themselves, only aversion and hatred—that's what is called the devil.

Luc Pascal wanted to bow me down, I think, humiliate me, there was a great deal of malice in him of which he was not in control. I certainly hated him because of Jacques, but I could not resist him.

I had refused to leave Jacques. I had refused to go away from Geneva even for an hour. I had refused everything. He understood that he had taken the wrong path, so he wounded my soul. Because Jacques had come back sick, with a fever, he wanted to stop me from taking care of Jacques. Unable to have me for himself, he captured me violently through pleasure. The last days before I went back to the bank were hell, I ran from one to the other. All of a sudden he left for Paris; I was alone with Jacques.

XXIX

I no longer leave Jacques, I do only a part of my job at the bank, I take care of him, he is sick.

I would like to say prayers over him. I would like . . . No, I have tortured myself, actually. I am completely humiliated, and I have the hope that I will regain my innocence. The fact is I want to die in order to begin again. That is what is happening inside me.

When I felt that I wasn't dying, that this was still Baladine, I was so desperate that I couldn't even go near his bed anymore.

His suffering was the link between us, and that could be a division.

I hurl myself in all directions to help him, but how can this help be possible? Yet the woman who was his wife still has something to say to him. I would like to have new senses, a new form, new thoughts, a different name. I say to him, new sister. I am the new sister. The word "new" keeps coming back to my mind because I have felt that it is the true word. Jacques answered me, I assure you, with his troubled gaze. (No—between us there was no forgiveness.)

His heart being wounded and sick, I struck at it. Sin was not what one should have said, one had to say crime. I entered into this idea of crime. I wanted to confess in detail my inner ignominy. Happily, he continued to look at me with his troubled gaze, and this kept me from the excesses I was about to commit.

The feeling of being miserable was what gave me back my love for him. I was less hemmed in and unhappy when I felt that I was going to be able to love him again. I was less desirous of punishment when a certain warmth returned.

In loving Jacques again, I recovered my own nature, which is to be confident, to want, always to go beyond pain, even the pain I have caused. Jacques was getting better. I wanted to be very bold and run every risk. I approached him closer and closer, silent, absolutely silent. At that point he could have thrust me away forever. No. One evening I really put my arms around him, he loved me. I thought I had triumphed over evil.

XXX

More than a month had passed since Ongero, and autumn was coming. At that time he spent a great deal on his clothes, everything I could give him. He became very elegant, but with an abandon that one couldn't help admiring. You know, he was tall, and, when his mood was calm, almost handsome. It was as though he had put his youth and what remained to him of insouciance into his homespun suits of very pretty colors, mauves or grays, with large pants; and also into stout leather shoes, delicate socks, a striped tie badly tied in a small knot around his silk collar. Alas! I thought: in these clothes, who is he? Jacques wandering, Jacques lazy, Jacques smoking—that's all. Well, to see him so handsome in his useless clothes made me weep.

If my tears came in his presence, he would not try to comfort me; he would leave the room.

It wasn't right away that I understood the thing that went along with this elegance. Shouldn't I have thought of it sooner? (Taddeo, hand in glove with him, bound by the same secrets but much too fastidious, did not accompany Jacques to those women where one found everything one could desire.) According to Taddeo, Jacques was looking for distraction. Jacques was forgetting those incidents, etc. So it was that Taddeo told me (something I took for a stroke of cruelty): "Baladine, he told me the other day that he would like to marry you."

When he came back *from there* at two or three o'clock in the morning, I had been waiting for him, I looked at him. He had on him some filthy thing. Or was my heart imagining it? I was alone, just me in front of him, and he was not alone at all: horrible creatures were in his hands, clinging to him, to his face, in his voice when he spoke. I was so afraid of letting myself be invaded by aversion that I made myself humble, small; and what was more, my faults also returned to my memory.

In October he began going to church again; he was seen at the services at Saint Peter's. Did he believe? What strange, contradictory acts! I myself cannot imagine Jacques's religion, I see nothing religious in him. He is sensitive, in love with things, he has no belief in a supernatural world. At Saint Peter's he could meet his father, his aunt, and other people of that sort; he met them, for I learned through Taddeo that he had written to the pastor to ask his forgiveness and requesting him to be so kind as to receive him at "Meadows" again. Thus Jacques, refusing to make peace in his heart, tried to be at peace with everyone else. He went there, to his father's home (at the time I knew nothing about it), and the hypocrites played out the scene of the Prodigal Son very well; it was enough in character for them. Even Taddeo was mistaken; he imagined that the letter written to the pastor had remained unanswered.

During the same period in which, without our being able to follow him, he was going somewhere, he demanded a great deal of me when I was with him. I had to be "beautiful, radiant." He oversaw my toilette very closely, bought my makeup, said I had to be "an active temptation to men and women." I asked for the afternoon off in order to go for a walk with him, I was so tired anyway. We went along the lake beyond Versoix to enjoy the last of the fine days—to look at the dead leaves of shrubs that fell in little coves and from there went drifting out into the open water.

XXXI

Taddeo and two friends had organized themselves to keep watch over Jacques (which proves, doesn't it, that Taddeo knew and feared something I did not suspect at all: there had been a conversation in which Jacques had said, like a religious crank, that as the adventure of his life was off on a false track, he had to present himself to God in a state of faith "in order to have unity"). So one or another of those young people always went with him, or followed him at a distance, or waited for him at an agreed-upon rendezvous somewhere.

On November 7 I returned from the bank with a migraine

headache and went to bed at six o'clock in the evening. He wasn't at the house. I fell asleep; but you know about that painful, terrible sleep, full of ghosts, in which you look for something, you don't recognize either yourself or anything anymore, you ask yourself with horror if you are real or not real, and as it happens I woke up a little clearer but only fell immediately back into the darkness and nausea. Sitting on my bed, I felt great discomfort: I was searching for Jacques with my hands and made the effort to recover his name. Knowing he was absent, I called him so that he would come in from the other room, and it was Taddeo who appeared.

Taddeo, surprised to see me sick, kind, arranging my pillows, wanted absolutely to tell me something, not in order to alarm me, but because what he would do next depended on my answer. Had I seen Jacques? No. Had he left a note here? I had so much trouble answering. No. Taddeo disappeared, saying he would be back at midnight. Why at midnight? I wasn't capable of putting things in their places, and I remember standing to go look out at the rue des Aubépines and Taddeo, who had left the house and was running off. The light was turned on and Taddeo stood before me; it was midnight. Taddeo was saying, "Listen Baladine." If he was talking this way, it was certainly so that I should not become more worried. I was very small in the corner of my nightmare as I listened to him.

"Listen, Baladine, I don't think Jacques will be back here tonight because he was seen at eleven o'clock leaving from Kursaal, in a car, with some friends. What friends we don't know."

"Where is he now?"

"We don't know, but friends are making telephone calls."

"What friends? Why telephone calls?" Oh, how unhappy I was!

"In order to find out, Baladine Nikolaievna, we have to find out."

Taddeo went out, came back in.

"We're going there right now and we'll bring him back."

"Where?"

"He's on the Willows Path, under the Rhône cliffs."

"What kind of weather is it out?"

"Don't worry, Baladine dear, it's possible he won't be here till morning. Sleep, sleep peacefully."

Down there near the Rhône a house was leaning. Jacques appeared on the road whistling a very cheerful tune. He was as pretty as a child with his pink cheeks and his wavy light hair. He approached the house, which was going to fall, completely unconcerned, and yet he was pointing to it. But then I discovered that Taddeo and all his friends were standing on the other side of the house, and, bracing themselves against the Rhône cliffs, were pushing so that the house would collapse on Jacques just at the right moment. I understood the plan; I set my back against the facade and, endowed with Herculean strength, I stopped everything. I had such a bad headache that day that Jacques said to me, "Go on behind the house with them." I refused, but he forced me by looking at me in a certain way only the two of us knew; and suddenly the house showed itself in its true nature, it was the Ongero church. Then there was nothing more to be done. Jacques was giving the orders. Taddeo pushed, with his gang, and I added my immense strength, which always decided everything. The church fell on Jacques, we saw Jacques with his arms to the sky and disappearing, and his eyes so unhappy between two stones in the vortex. Then the scene suddenly changed, I was in the sea, as at Odessa when I was little, and I was swimming.

XXXII

I woke up at dawn and my migraine was gone. As though someone had emptied my heart of the false anguish and put the real one into it.

At seven o'clock I rang Taddeo's doorbell; he had gone off again very early (at five o'clock in the morning). I went back home. Taddeo was waiting for me. I threw myself at him. "We have him," he said.

He kissed me and I kissed him. "Dear Baladine, he will be back home with you this afternoon, let's not rush things too much." Oh! I felt all this was so serious that I didn't dream of questioning it. Taddeo's hand was trembling as he held a cigarette; he noticed it, threw away the cigarette, plunged his hand into his pocket. "He was in a wretched state, he's better now."

Taddeo now talked only about my health, smiling awkwardly, and I, remembering the bad dream during the night, blushed at each of his remarks. The dear boy. "I will stay and have lunch with you and we will prepare everything so that his return will be happy."

At three o'clock Jacques came back. What a face!

Under his eyes two gray circles speckled with black spots. His mouth pulled to one side by the smile he was trying to produce. A smile for whom? I took his hand and immediately laid my head on his shoulder; I stayed there with my eyes closed. It was imprudent on my part. Too bad.

He said, with feeble roughness, "So what's the fuss about?" and again, "What's the fuss about?" However, I did not lift my head; he did not back off. "What's the fuss about?" How unfeeling he was, without pity, and no honesty! "Look, nothing happened to me. I didn't hurt anyone, I went for a walk." "What a lot of fuss! I went for a walk."

We served the tea. By this time I suspected every possible thing.

Abruptly—oh, what madness! Jacques kicked a chair and burst out laughing. "Ah! The cows!" He swore, and began laughing again, harder. "I was on the quay, I was following two fashionable ladies near Mont Blanc Palace," more laughing,

laughing. "One was saying to the other: 'Oh, a woman's life! It's a never-ending battle against unwanted hair.'" He laughed. Taddeo laughed. I did too, we were caught up in it.

Idiotic laughter, you understand, a discharge of laughter. In that laughter we could laugh and cry, mixed up together.

Jacques was sunk in an armchair. As he laughed he showed his big teeth, and because his skin was drawn with fatigue, it looked as though his jaw were jutting out of his face, and his pale, exhausted eyes, the eyes of unhappiness, were shining with pleasure at the same time. He swung his head as he planted jokes. Everything passed by, it was a parade, us and the others: Geneva with our wretched life. We laughed so much we were avenged. His laughter forces him to laugh, but he is still sad, gloomy. Taddeo plays the smart aleck; as for me, I'm nasty. What laughter! It seemed to me my heart was being flayed.

We vilified everything: the Bible, the Comburgers of Combourg, his father, whom he called the Apostle of Meadows, and his Aunt Angèle the ladybug, me at the Bank of the Last Judgment, him at a reunion with his former classmates—I'm telling you all this—in sum, the absurd behavior of every person in this nasty town, and ours, for we were not spared. And soon he stood up, a sort of jovial madman, and set about insulting Luc Pascal's image, he tore it to shreds, he displayed his defects and his cowardices; it was as though he were destroying a stuffed doll. I was still laughing. I was laughing with all my teeth showing, and my hair tossed back. And I must have been lovely laughing so heartily, but it was as though I, too, were destroying my stuffed doll: so much pain, so much pain, and laughter.

XXXIII

(We see Jacques at the Café du Nord.
He leaves his friends in the downstairs room, goes up the

staircase, enters the toilet, immediately leaves again by way of the tradesmen's hallway; here he is outside the service entrance. It was nicely done. Bareheaded and without an overcoat. A November night. Tip-top. Djag-rag.

He walks onto the Rhône quay, proceeds along it at a quick pace. He begins running a hundred yards before the Pont-en-l'Ile. No one in the streets. It is almost midnight and the north wind is blowing.

After the bridge he continues along the quay—farther. He speaks out loud in order to express the surge of his thoughts. I am strong, it is cold. Why did I wait until tonight? How long it took to find myself! The door I have to go through is narrow. The hard and abject door is narrow. It is not real. On the other side will be what I desire. God, you have given me this great desire. God, you know yourself in my desire. My life was division without God and tonight I form the Oneness.

I must go on without failing in order to reach the other side. Because on the side where we are everything is broken and spoiled. My friends, I have nothing more to do in this place, as the law has been transgressed. *Now I must arrive*, and quickly: I have an infinite hope.

At the highest point of his being, in order to succeed in being no longer. "We will see afterward." It's funny, the determination not to be anymore. He is going to die. Djag.

We see Jacques looking at the Rhône.

An electric light casts Jacques's shadow on the quay. The river is black, swollen, a fearsome current, the temperature of the water is four or five degrees, not more. Fortunately my stomach is stuffed from a good dinner with my friends at the Café du Nord. Djag.

A play of water memories. "Summer morning . . . the bathing place of the handsome young men, swimming, the sun, swimming . . . All the flowers, all the birds." Vermala on the mountain. From Vermala, the river one sees in the valley is the

Rhône. That sun will never appear. First appearance of Baladine, first appearance of Luc. "June morning, all the flowers, all the birds. I know how to be happy like no one else in the world." Second appearance of Baladine: the funicular. New appearance of Baladine: at Lausanne. "A child with bare feet." Charles. Charles Stoebli. The hut in the pasture, Charles, happiness. No!—Come now, peace in there, all of you! Quiet, characters [and you pretend death doesn't frighten you]—well yes, well no—quiet, characters! or in ten minutes I'm nabbed by Taddeo and his gang. I already told you you had to *stay good and calm* because *you don't know about* what is going to happen. So it's outrageous, good.

Oh, I don't care about them! I don't care about them! I don't care about them!—You really think a person can unhook his soul from his nerve machine without suffering?

You're right.

Well there's my native city, my mother city; the black wind is piercing it to the bones, and good-bye. Parapet. High enough.

Well, I will think of Him with my last thought as a man, of Him only, since this is for Him: he sees how I am acting in this hour. He judges. He pardons me? I wouldn't dare. He has put this desire in me, he is helping me. He whispers to me the order to obey. I don't know anymore. I can't fear You because I am looking for You, I can fear only myself because I am a sinner and full of anguish, so I give myself to You as a sacrifice in order that You judge me and that You make Your dominion in me for eternity if You want. I ask You to forgive me for my weak love, but when love for You came back, it wasn't my love, it was Yours, and since it came from You I have confidence, absolute confidence. I am fully confident for the time of eternity.

This is the right spot. Ed. Schütz Jeweler, Clockmaker, Optical Instruments. Jump. The poor boy doesn't like it. Come on, jump. Heavy heart. *Very tranquil* mind.

Cause grief to . . . Baladine, I loved you. I pardon you completely. You allow me to leave, you pardon me, good.

Taddeo, dear fellow, you did what you had to. Your hand, and let me go.

No, my love, it's good, go on, good, good and calm and necessary, completely good. Don't cry, bride. No, my love, it's good, go on. Ah—I see her in the water the way I used to when I was a kid.

Beautiful. Spiritual. Lily of the Sky. Go with me.

I believe in God.

Button my jacket. My wallet is in the rubber envelope. They'll find it. Good and calm.

There, easy now.

—It's—Ooh—.)

XXXIV

On the night of November 12 he disappeared. He was in the café with them. He must have escaped through the little door; they never knew. Taddeo thought he was in the toilet, and when he decided to go see, no one was there. Taddeo was at my place before midnight. I got up, I went with him. Just looking at Taddeo I understood: misfortune had struck.

They had gone along the quays because they knew his idea was the water.

We met again in front of the café he took off from. Taddeo had pulled himself together and was making speeches to me, but I myself was sure. We didn't dare go to the police yet. We had to do something, do something. What could we do? It was impossible for us to separate. I asked them to come back to my place, to see. At the rue des Aubépines, Taddeo decided: let's go to the police. In order to find some sort of support, because one couldn't stay that way, just the four of us, carrying the weight of his death. Taddeo roused the police, went in. They called us, too. The police didn't know anything, and they didn't seem to be taking the thing seriously. I said to them, he's dead. They said to me, calm down, Madame. I'm sure his soul was communicating with me to let me know he was dead.

We returned to the rue des Aubépines and then once again to the banks of the Rhône. We were drawn there. I recall clearly where it was, in front of Schütz the jeweler. The water was terrible, the north wind was blowing furiously. We remained there, huddled against one another. We were not crying and we were not speaking either. We no longer thought of going to look for him anywhere. Now they were sure, like me. I looked at the water and thought about him as a creature too beautiful to have been real. I did not say to myself: he threw himself into the water, into this water, he is somewhere at the bottom, I will never see him again. I thought: how magnificent was the dream that I made of him, here and elsewhere! I would never live with that dream again, through my own fault, and they took me back home.

Why tell about the other days? If you want me to I will describe them to you. The next day the pastor came to my place, informed by the police. Taking both my hands in his as though I were a child, he begged me to find Jacques. We telephoned all over, the police were looking for Jacques de Todi, and the pastor went to the offices of the newspapers to ask them to say nothing about the disappearance of his son. The following day still nothing. I kept saying: leave his body to sleep where it is. They did not listen to me, naturally. Telegrams were sent to Luc Pascal, to Siemens, even to the hotels in Vermala. Taddeo had a man whom he used as a model and who worked as an electrician at the Pont de la Coulouvrenière. This man came on November

15 and said, "Feeling I got is there's something in the grating in front of the sluices, so I wanted to let you know before the police," and Taddeo went there without saying anything to me. An enormous body whose proportions did not in the least correspond to Jacques was indeed lying against the grating, and they saw it better and better. The police were alerted immediately after, but Taddeo still did not say anything to me, thinking that it wasn't Jacques. I would have declared, it's him. They fished out the body and Taddeo had to examine it. Taddeo recognized Jacques's shoes and the gold buttons on the cuffs of his shirt. Next they found his wallet, wrapped in rubber, which he had placed in the lining of his vest. The papers could still be read. I was informed. The body was in the amphitheater of the hospital and I should not see it. Taddeo had said to me, "There's no point, there's nothing left of him."

The wallet contained a note "For Baladine" that read: "To my dear departed wife, forgive me." Another paper, his will, in which he left me his manuscripts and the canvases he had painted. A whole letter for his father: he wrote that he was stopping a monstrous life in order to allow his better being to continue, that he believed in God, and that he was expecting to find himself again in the Oneness. This letter was very beautiful. Another note for me, written earlier, perhaps at the moment of his first flight, was full of extremely tender, intimate, and sensual things, with oddities—mysterious, so discontinuous that I still haven't uncovered all its meanings even today. Yet not a day goes by that I do not reread this piece of paper.

For Taddeo, too, there was a note, even one for Luc Pascal: "I repent having made fun of Luc when I had already decided to leave this world."

I followed Jacques's procession beside Pastor Isaac de Todi, and Taddeo was behind us. There was a religious service at Saint Peter's. Jacques's body was burned.

[END OF BALADINE'S STORY]

90

PART TWO

The Frost

I

....

XXXV

Time
Mornings years
It's nice out it's overcast it's ugly
Hopes and returns
One wouldn't believe that the depth of the lake is diminishing
Certain people disappear
One wouldn't believe there are so many dead in the streets
Because of the war
One sees the mountain out one's window
One wouldn't believe it is still such a rose color or so green
Evil is universal
One wouldn't believe all this could last so long
Sorrow is particular
Age is a little more dangerous when it comes
The mirror
Each day is added to the column
Thoughts hurt at five o'clock in the evening
The seasons are pretty bad
The winds from all quarters

Things have certainly changed anyway
Thus children grow uninterruptedly
The sun appears in the morning
And men seek pleasure
Novelties
The sun obliterates a delirium one has toward four o'clock in
    the morning

That is, it pours a narcotic for the day
The breeze comes and insists and recalls a lost love
Then the sun sets and the delirium takes over

Business is great 400%
Geneva is in its place at the end of the lake
The number of the year is 1919
People dance
The number of the age is 41 years
The joys of men are as horrible as their pains
One doesn't understand the heavens
An Abdullah cigarette—let's go

XXXVI

Baladine Nikolaievna noticed him, at last distinctly himself, on the sidewalk of the Corraterie, as her hand touched the door of her bank.

He was waiting for her at five minutes to two.

Wasn't she ready for this? For several days he had been present without showing himself. Baladine put out her hand and smiled bravely. I smile like the sky, for no one in particular.

Luc Pascal had not aged much. Not quite the same in her case, right?

"I don't have any time at all to talk to you."

"Today it's enough for me to see you again."

"Good-bye."

"You didn't answer my letters, that's why I'm here."

"Excuse me, I did answer you."

"Two very odd lines."

"I wrote you: Baladine, Baladine and her child, are at home at number 32, route de Conches, after seven in the evening. It was an invitation."

"I'll come."

"Tomorrow, if you like."

He shook her hand while she smiled at a vague horizon. Her eyes still have circles around them and there are her eyelashes. She went into her office.

"See you soon?"

The catastrophe in Europe had upset everything without touching a single personal sorrow, without changing a single secret life.

In 1919 Baladine Nikolaievna Sergounine was still living in Geneva, she was still at the Union du Crédit Suisse. Baladine had a child, Pierrot, born June 20, 1914, and the child bore the name of Todi.

Until 1916, Taddeo Buonvicini had remained Baladine's faithful friend with whom she could still talk about Jacques; nothing had prevented him from going off to enlist in Italy, and he had disappeared almost right away, on the Carso.

She lived alone with her child and some cats, in a house in Conches surrounded by tall pine trees. It was pleasant in the summer, damp in the winter. She knew no one, her life being, in the eyes of virtuous Geneva, a model of scandal for several reasons.

At the bank, at least, she held a very enviable position because of fine qualities she had displayed.

No news from anywhere.

But all that did not really exist. Baladine was an empty creature, alienated, and empty without even feeling her unhappiness.

At present her hair was a little gray, silvered, in contrast to her face, which had remained naturally rosy. That gray hair, short and curly, was still proud. But neither powder nor make-up, no shining veil over her eyes, her skin clean and rather sad. Her eyes were larger, a blue area extended them into the flesh of her cheeks. Yet was everything lost for her? One noticed a touch of burning tenderness near her mouth, which was still naive. That was why men still turned around when Baladine Nikolaievna went by.

XXXVII

Her son was a blue-eyed, blond-haired youngster, "and beyond that what do I know about him? Nothing at all." Strangely absentminded—"are you an angel fallen down to earth by mistake and will you ever manage to do something useful, my dear?"—affectionate and a bit of a scamp, obeying out of mischievousness; "his aim is to escape you always" and "one can never hold onto him." "What I'm saying is I'm not cut out to be a mother, obviously I love him, maybe through my intellect, as I have no passion." She was down-to-earth, enumerated the resemblances. "His hooded eyes would come from Grandfather Sergounine, his blond hair from his father, all the rest from me. Well, no, that resemblance about the eyes is dubious, and Jacques's hair was as soft as his is frizzy." "He came out of me and he is my object (pride, jealousy), but I am such a funny woman, I don't care." Yet she lived only for Pierrot from six o'clock in the evening on; she hung on his movements.

She remembered the birth and her horror (Jacques's child after Jacques's death). "But now that he's growing, it's indifference."

"Unless he actually saved me?"

"If I died, anyone at all could take charge of him and bring him up, it would be just as good."

"I am so little his mother."

XXXVIII

This Baladine, walking on dry stones, thirsty, not noticing any cultivated land, any live plant, burned and looking for shade, this Baladine, fiery and empty, truly has only one reason for walking: Jacques's child, who is here. He fiddles about in the shade of the garden, delaying with a thousand tricks the moment of going to sleep, this little stranger whom I kiss and whom I made, this cruel child who likes to torture insects when he can catch them, who smiles mysteriously at the moon in the dark sky.

"Pierrot, go to bed."

"Yes, Mama."

"Kiss me."

"I'm coming, Mama."

"Kiss me one more time, will you?"

He kisses her like a little lover, with deliberation and making the pleasure last.

"Now off with you."

She is alone.

Baladine scarcely thought about it during the hot afternoon, sitting at her desk in the yellow shade of the large awning. Well, so Luc Pascal has come back. He wants to see me again. He understood my answer perfectly well, that I didn't have any intention of having him come visit *so quickly*. Baladine had too much to do between two and six o'clock with all sorts of difficulties on the lines from London, Zurich, and South America; she dictated fourteen letters, wrote or transmitted items of information:

Steels discussed: Steel *gained 5/8*, Cast Iron Pipe *achieved another sensational rise of 11 1/4 points, while* Bethlehem *lost 1/8*, Crucible *gave up 1/4 and* Baldwin *1/2;* American Locomotive *gained 3/4.*

LENA GOLDFIELDS.—*At Lenskoi mine, during the week of July 8–15, 7,999 cubic yards were extracted and 12,480 cubic yards washed. 8,295 ounces of gold were obtained, valued at 34,839 pounds sterling . . .*

She didn't have a second more for her own life and Luc Pascal. Can Luc Pascal see that Baladine is as much a businesswoman in the practice of her life as she is empty inside? As this useless machinery of life must necessarily go on running, well then, let it yield, let it give things, things that give us pleasure, let it amuse us. Baladine wants to believe only in things now, and in games with things. The bank's turnover has tripled since the hostilities ended; in the Geneva house, Baladine is in charge of a department, and if we have to be specific here too, with numbers, she is worth four times what she was worth before. You work, you invent, you buy; pleasures, comfort, and art come afterward. Baladine knows everything now; she knows that she has to put the money she earns into stock-market speculations, jewels, her tailor and dressmaker.

Now, on the way home, the idea resurfaced: Luc Pascal has come back. Baladine looked at the radiant sky, something that never happened to her anymore. She thought with tenderness of Pierrot back from the Oak School, waiting for her next to the gate; sentimental was what she was. She found Pierrot leaning his elbows on the gate. As she was combing his hair a little later—"Naughty boy! You've completely mussed up your hair, and what have you been up to, I'm finding bits of matchsticks, my dear?"—she thought: life is beginning again, life always begins again, one can't stop it, it's tiring. Then she combed her own hair carefully and changed her dress. From this moment on her mind was preoccupied by Luc Pascal.

There she is, alone in the dark garden. Pierrot, whom she is keeping an eye on, puts out his light and the window of his room disappears. She is cold even though the air is muggy. She says, "I'll go get a shawl," but this is a pretext for leaving the garden, which is too dark, too solitary.

Why is he coming back? What does he want? Why? Nothing is left of the past. I was there, yes; now I am here. This thing has so little importance. Time absorbs our little stories. I don't understand what he wants.

XXXIX

The next evening Luc entered her home as she was waiting for him with irritation and curiosity, and once again the vague terror of being alone.

A little ceremonious, surprised by the sadness of the place. (He doesn't like my "furnished apartment," he is startled to see an elegant woman here, he no doubt expected a little bourgeois life.) Well, here I am, how do I seem to you? Luc lost himself in compliments and Baladine said to him inwardly: "Come now, be straightforward my poor friend, the way I am myself. Why do you have to squirm like that?"

Luc's eyes, wandering to find some support, lighted on the mantlepiece ("yes, on the mantelpiece; it's pretty idiotic, isn't it, but I don't care about my apartment and I have no aesthetics") where two photographs were displayed: one showed Jacques smiling in the sun at Ongero, a snapshot taken by Luc that she had had enlarged; the other was a portrait by Boissonnas, Taddeo with his pretty silk scarf. Luc's eyes remained stuck like arrows on Jacques's image.

Then a magnetic influence occurred and they talked. Right away their remarks were serious. There was melancholy and more, but certainly not tenderness. I can't tolerate pity, Baladine's body announced—and I have no intention of offering you any, Luc answered.

Through an unexpected, tangible mechanism, she was discovering that Luc had changed profoundly. She did not know certain of his phrases or intonations. Physically the same, though more drawn, and his face shaved, whereas at Vermala (and at Ongero) he had sported a little mustache the breadth of his mouth. The change could be found, it seemed, in the power, the center, the connection between his physical aspects and others. "It will be quite difficult for me to become familiar with him again."

"Is your child asleep?"
"Do you smoke?" (She offered her Abdullahs.)
"Only Virginia tobacco in a pipe. What is that anyway?"
"English tobacco from the Orient. Fashionable."
"I'm not up to date."
Baladine smokes.
"He's asleep."
"I would have liked to see him."
"That will be for another time."
She could not have tolerated showing him asleep.
"What's his name?"
"Pierrot. Pierre de Todi."
"Is he nice?"
"Very."
"Show me a picture?"
"No, I don't have a picture, I don't have any, it's funny."
"I'll come back especially to see him."
"Yes, come back. At six o'clock."
"Are you happy to have him?"
"Well naturally, how odd you are, Pierrot is my whole life."
"Your whole life."
Baladine wanted to object to all these questions he was asking about her, about the child—if the child was intelligent—if the money they had was adequate—if she got along well with Pierrot. "And us? and I? do we belong to you? Our life has no value, but why should I deliver it up to you?" When he said to her, Do you get along well with Pierrot? she found the question insulting and wanted to hurl something insolent at him, any-

100

thing at all, to make him leave. However, she smiled like a disconsolate angel. Sitting down, she made her bust dance slightly as though she were hearing jazz. She answered all the questions. "You come back from far away, my dear. What right have you? None." But she told him everything in spite of herself, and when she thought, "This time, no, that's enough, I'm not saying another word, it's up to him to talk, I want that," she continued to give in, to advance toward him while he did not budge. It is too strong! Already they knew each other a little better. Baladine looked at her new friend. One felt a spirit radiating around his forehead, and Baladine, because she was becoming attentive to many things, no longer had anything unpleasant in her thoughts, no upsurge of amour propre, and also no more of the gratuitous, stupid coquetry she had at first shown at the door of the bank. Her irritation dropped away, whatever there had been of it; with a naive gesture of her hand, which bore a large black ring, she lifted the gray hair the evening wind had drawn over her forehead, the better to see, the better to grasp, Luc's presence.

XL

"Life has turned out to be unkind to me, Baladine, not that it has overwhelmed me with particular misfortunes, but because at each instant it *forces* me to accept what my freedom finds intolerable. For twenty years I have been engaged in a process of breaking away. As a child, my life was like the wall that cast its shadow over the courtyard of the house, an enormous, damp wall without light; my father, a provincial notary, beat my mother before my eyes. As an adolescent, I experienced love through onanism, then through a long adulterous affair (with the mother of one of my friends). As a man, I am not loved, I don't manage to get married, and for health reasons I go to brothels. When that revolts me too much, I become a monk for six months, but then 'anger is my normal condition.' I carry within me a mad desire for beauty and infinitude: I achieve almost nothing of it in my days. My work encounters no favor, not one success. I met Jacques in 1909. At Ongero I dealt him the worst blow he had ever received. The war and what followed have almost affected my judgment: but this is another story. I've found you again and here we are, face to face with each other.

"I did not accept Jacques's death.

"I do not accept it. I don't want it to have happened, I don't want it to be. I try to prevent it, or else, turning in a different direction, I have to find a meaning for it. I have to see its active value in what I call life. But no, nothing; no value, no beauty. How can I admit that a man so rare, endowed with all the gifts, one of the elect, killed himself—either because he was disappointed in love or because he felt a desire different from that of most men? Jacques was a wonderful child, nothing was decided for him, nothing written in advance, nothing excluded. There was nothing abnormal in him: then what would be forbidden to the rest of us? We pay pretty dearly for life and do a pretty pure work on this planet. And lastly, from Jacques to me, between Jacques and me, there is you.

"What happened, listen to me carefully, is that throughout the events of the last few years, the public calamity and my personal ordeals, I have remained locked up with Jacques, yes, alone with him, contemplating him and searching for him, tied to his ghost—as I said, locked up with him. And the prison the two of us were in was the memory I had of you, your image. It's quite complicated. Because I couldn't endure the reality of Jacques's death, that suicide, in which I played a part, had to be obliterated through an operation of my mind, or perhaps by a soothing and magical operation on your part. I beg you not to think I'm sick, because I reason perfectly well in all circumstances, and I can distinguish between what could be called disturbed about my condition (difficulties, distresses) and, on the other hand, a very penetrating attempt in my thoughts to assimilate the death. A certain eternal pain, whose nature is unknown to me, exists between him and me, and it must find its resolution. Where? In my own death? I considered that. But that evasion on my part, by displacing the whole problem into the unknown, does not satisfy my mind. Reparation with respect to Jacques, Jacques's salvation, ought primarily to be achieved in me and in us on this earth, as we were when he died. In 1915 and 1916 my thoughts remained firm, but the spellbound condition in which Jacques was maintaining me was expressed by considerable physical discomfort. I cured myself by making a pact between myself and Jacques's ghost, by making a commitment to find you again. I would have come back in 1918 if I had been able to. I didn't try to write to you about such a subject. Finally, for the last six months I have hesitated and several times I've turned back. What do we know about death, about our duty toward it, about its influence on our lives? No death will be more intolerable for me than Jacques's. It's up to us to soothe what is still suffering in him.

"I am so happy to have found you again."

XLI

She answered, "I have trouble following you in your thinking, this is obscure and uncertain for me." She added: "But I'm very moved. You know, I'm a woman entirely in this world here, unhappy and empty perhaps, but about the rest I don't know, I don't understand, I believe that when one dies everything is finished. And yet you unsettle me. In relation to Jacques, I was the best wife, and the worst. Really, I never ask myself questions. Because there was Jacques, I consent to see you again.

We will be for each other what you like. I think I can still be a friend to you. You will see that I'm a creature without any other usefulness. I don't think I still love you."

Luc Pascal became acquainted with Pierrot.

The weapons are not equal. Luc, trembling, seeks the truth, and other things besides. Pierrot pays no attention to this bald man whom he has never seen before, but gives his mother a more intense look and escapes. Seeing the boy walking on the path, he recognizes Jacques—thinks he recognizes him.

He had never known how to speak to a child. The attitude of this one, unsociable and disdainful, is set and will not change. Pierrot, always polite as one is on a walk, does not talk to or look in the direction of the stranger. When Baladine says to him, "Come here," he comes up. "Give your hand to our friend Monsieur Luc." He gives it and withdraws it in the same motion.

"Pierrot, you're not being nice."

"Yes I am, Mama."

If he has a story to tell, it is for his mother, and if he happens to find himself with Monsieur Luc, after an instant Monsieur Luc is alone.

Pierrot, looking at the stranger, imperceptibly drifts toward his mother; he comes to her, buries his head in her breast, and wraps his arms around her waist. "How loving you are, my dear!" Baladine yields to this offensive of affection out of habit. Flattered, too, in front of Luc and pursuing—who knows?—another feeling that is slipping away. Anyway, can this youngster be taken seriously, I ask you? Neither for the child nor for Luc should one appear to be moved.

But it is remarkable that Luc is immediately bitten by a mad jealousy, and that when the little scene begins again, he is obliged to stand, pick up his hat, and, invoking a random pretext, go away. Baladine sees his suffering. By this Luc understands what he has not wanted to grasp until now.

That loving approach of the child teaches Luc that he cannot fulfill his vow without loving Baladine completely, and just as much with his senses as with his affections or mind; otherwise the old constellation will form again: a Jacques armed with all the rights thrusting Luc away, and Luc once again becoming vicious, an abductor. "The mysterious operation that I want to perform with Jacques, of our eternal friendship, requires that I include his son and that I recapture the whole of Baladine's heart." But how should he love Baladine?

However, he dared say to her, "Baladine, as God is your witness, is this really Jacques's child?"

"Yes, he is Jacques's child."

XLII

When Baladine gave herself to Luc Pascal again, this time in the full freedom of her life, it was in August, still in the house at Conches. On a strange evening when the sky was a ceramic blue, when the house appeared to stand aligned with the edge of the road that was still red, and tall trees pointed their dark tips upward.

Storms rumbled in the distance. Through the dark square of the open window they heard the crickets, which make their tranquil noise until after midnight.

Baladine had not in the least wanted to undress—like a traveler who is going to be leaving again for good. Conquered, she said to herself, why should I hide myself? She took off all her clothes.

This statue who heavily moves her upturned breasts. Luc,

closing his eyes in love, waited for the miracle that the highest of melancholy days must bring. All three united, joined and reconciled. In the melancholy of the beautiful, eternal day.

XLIII

Baladine strides with her lively morning legs toward the city, toward her bank. The weather fresh and fine, the day crystalline. When she passes from sun to shade and from shade to sun, she sighs, or she sings, or she says: "If we have happiness, here, happiness, let the crick crunch me, as Pierrot says. But it's never happiness that one seeks." Now she is under the trees. "Everything is beautiful. I've done the right thing, he's done the right thing. My lovely morning, I am a little girl and I'm going off to look for flowers in the meadow, that's all! Why, look, I've gone down a new road, I should have made a wish. For what? (Poor Taddeo, when he said to me, 'Sergounine, you are superstitious.') Of course I'm superstitious! I wish—for him to keep his young heart." Then she analyzes: "Is your wish for you or for him? Here you are at your age, as selfish as a woman of twenty. I'm a woman infatuated. Captivated, infatuated. How everything has changed! I'm almost happy." And again: "I'm waiting. No, I'm not waiting for anything anymore. It's true, I'm not waiting for anything anymore." She is surprised. "Ah! I'm almost happy. I'm young, I'm cheerful, I'm sad, I'm old, I'm young. This morning I'm really very cheerful and very young. Even so, pain is good, life is worth the trouble. We're up high, we're down low, we love each other. It's good. It's so good! How do I love him? If I had a daisy to pluck the petals off: a little a lot passionately." Not having a daisy scares her. "Fear is always there, I don't want to look at it anymore, I don't want to. I don't want to be afraid of loving, I don't want to anymore. Will I love him for a long time? Will it always be good like today? He will be free, so he will remain a true child. I will be free, too. One mustn't hesitate in one's answers, that brings unhappiness. How beautiful it is, how beautiful it is in my heart and in the sky!"

The Florissant road does actually appear, rose-colored with blue edges. It deserves its name because of the beautiful perfumes that pass over it, coming from the pines, the beds of flowers, wild oats. The perfumes come, they surround the passing woman who walks quickly (without losing anything of the forms or lights), and Baladine opens her parasol. The estates behind their enclosures are at once forbidden and inviting; on a lawn one sees an old Genevois gentleman taking his "constitutional" while inspecting his trees.

As she arrives at the outskirts of the city, thinking of the old gentleman, suddenly her soul collapses, this is something else. To flee, to run away, alone, down this warm road, despite the sun, despite the birds; or through those streets. Take off and leave everything and, most of all, abandon what she loves, alone, alone, having only her parasol and her handbag with a little money. Go to France, plunge into Paris, become a kept woman or anything at all, but lose herself there, lose herself, lose herself!

Baladine ran in Geneva, not understanding what evil was afflicting her, and she called to Luc to help her. Luc, my love, my friend, Luc, and she blotted her tears with her glove. She kept hearing (an obsession) Luc saying to her at Lucerne, "You're like a Renoir."

II

....

XLIV

The events that constitute the end of this story, as much by the slowness of their unfolding over several years as by their strictly interior nature, exterior manifestations being uncertain or ill attuned to the internal reality because of the fictitious aspect of this tragedy from which one of the protagonists is missing, have seemed improbable to a few of those persons who, by forcing their way into the secret, were able to approach Luc Pascal as a writer during the last and most active part of his literary life. Nevertheless, its reality could not be more certain, for it is established by the notes of Pascal himself.

But let us first describe the facts that came before, and that form a door to the new life.

XLV

At noon on May 16, 1921, the marriage of Luc and Baladine was celebrated at the city hall in Geneva. A civil marriage with two required witnesses: a male friend of the groom, a young lady in the profession of stenographer for the bride. Baladine Nikolaievna Sergounine, Russian subject, divorced wife of Reinhardt, married Luc-Marie Pascal, man of letters in Paris, the domicile of the married couple in Geneva being the Lake Hotel.

However unimportant this act might have seemed to the married couple, registering as it did a union that had been in effect for more than a year, when Baladine Pascal reappeared on the front steps, married, it seemed that her shoulders, the attentiveness of her face, her beautiful, somewhat more slender figure, the gravity of her eyes, gave her a very moving quality. Luc Pascal seemed equally happy, but as preoccupied as his wife seemed momentarily free of worry, often stealing a look at her with an air quite different from the one he assumed when he smiled at her. The husband and wife returned to the Lake Hotel twenty minutes after leaving it. A little later Madame Baladine Pascal could be seen in her everyday suit, for at about two o'clock she resumed her work as usual.

Those at the Union du Crédit Suisse bank who knew her related "how he had visited her in a villa at Conches, but they had had to leave that place because their relationship was causing a scandal and they were receiving anonymous letters, especially as a child existed who was her natural son, and besides, this harked back to another story, the story of *Jacques de Todi* the pastor's son, who had mysteriously committed suicide, and with whom this woman Baladine had also lived." All this does not mean that a woman with such a past could not be outstanding in business matters, as she gave proof of it every day! "Oh, what lives these foreigners lead! I myself could never," said a young lady from Plainpalais who worked in the accounts department.

Could public opinion know how meaningless an act this odd marriage was? Meaningless for the two, who not only are a true couple but find themselves joined together "for better for worse" by bonds much older and of a fearful nature, which they neither could nor wished to explain.

The fact that they had breathed the same air, slept the same sleep, and known the same pleasure was almost nothing to them, but that the same moan of extreme anguish could be transferred from one to the other, or the light of hope, that one and the same evil particular to them was known to each of them and accepted; on the other hand, that everything in him, even if misunderstood by her, had to pass through her, and that every force in her sought its echo in him—this was what gave the morning's ceremony, as ceremony, an almost odious absurdity.

Ten years of full and grave secrets stood behind them. On Saint Peter's Square, which they had crossed, a well-loved ghost (a hated ghost) had touched their joined hands before returning to the heavens, its terrible domain.

XLVI

Then why this distress of Baladine's in her room, before she puts on her suit? This absolute distress: she is sobbing in the middle of the room, her head buried in her hands and her body thrown on a couch.

Luc (insensitive to this sort of despair anyway) did not hear her, because she was making so little noise. He was in the large room next door, high-ceilinged, padded door. She could see him through that door: the only power that had remained hard in a fog of derision. Standing in front of the table and continuing the sorting of papers begun the day before, a sorting that will be finished by the departure. He is motionless, closed, isolated as though in a shell, embedded in matter. Unkind? No, but without pity. Baladine's sobs redouble.

Someone is trying to enter from the hallway, the brass doorknob turns in vain: it's Pierrot. He doesn't insist, he goes off "to his papa."

Then she stood up, packed a bag hastily.

She stuffed the compartments with dresses, underclothes, Pierrot's clothes; she also took Luc's books. She worked as quickly as possible, but still picked through the child's things: what was indispensable, nice, superfluous. For her, only a dozen

111

essentials objects—portraits, photographs (Luc, Taddeo, and Jacques) that she crammed together in her underclothes. She stood in front of the dressing table, powdered her eyes, thought of nothing more.

She took off her black wedding dress, replacing it with a tailored brown serge suit. She opened the suitcase again because she had forgotten a yellowed lavender purse that came from Jacques's Aunt Angèle.

Then she pushed the suitcase under the couch, went out, met Pierrot in the corridor, and kissed him rapturously.

Luc joined them at the restaurant at about one fifteen. During lunch, Baladine said: "I'm going to the office, but I really think I'll find a mess there, and I'm afraid of being delayed tomorrow, my dear. Please leave for Brigue as we agreed. This evening. Pierrot and I will meet you there Saturday morning. Okay?"

Luc made several objections, tried to keep her with him that evening, felt a serious obstacle. He looked her straight in the face: "Whatever you like." He added, "I had arranged this little trip for you."

Baladine said, "I know."

"In any case, don't come later than Saturday."

They went out together into the rue du Rhône. "I'll probably be gone when you get back." Luc kissed Baladine. "Until Saturday, dear."

"Until Saturday."

And Baladine turned back three times toward her husband, who was moving away.

XLVII

In Brigue, in the Valais, there is a large cross.

One goes up a street beyond the Castle with its four copper

bulbs; one heads toward the mountain and the first meadows fenced by planks, but this is still in the town. One sees above a wall what is probably the chapel of a convent, which presents a flat facade ending in a gable like a tall abstract house. Up here is the cross.

Immense, the cross occupies two-thirds of the facade. Bare, it is without ornament. It is emblematic. Its wood pieces are slender; from a distance one would think one was looking at two sticks. It is not a cross on which one could crucify anyone. Not a bloody cross. It's a cross of thought, of love and metaphysics. A cross of eternal cause; of superior sorrow, power, joy; of abstraction of life and of self; of rejoining with the Spirit.

Luc Pascal, leaning against the alley wall, contemplates the cross.

First operation: self-concentration.

Second operation: emptiness and strength.

Third operation: humility, thirst.

To perform these operations, not to sleep anymore and to keep walking.

III

·······················

XLVIII

Luc Pascal had been abandoned on May 17, the very day after his marriage, by Baladine, who had made use of the trip to Brigue. The Lake Hotel telephoned that "Madame and the little boy had left Friday evening to catch a night train." Luc was in Geneva by Saturday. At the station he learned the details: train no. 668, departing at 9:30 P.M. for Paris. On Monday, Luc left Switzerland forever, traveling toward Paris in his turn.

He had no time to experience the horror of it, no time to be sad or even to worry, he was counting the clicking of the wheels on the rails; tomorrow morning he would be there, in Paris, he'd overtake her—of course he would find her again, and if she saw him just once, he was sure of getting her back.

Because when he had gone into the disheveled bedroom at the Lake Hotel (as though someone had been killed there), he had first seen the dresses on the floor (and devouring them with kisses, had recovered the scent of her sweat), then, in plain sight on the dressing table, an open copy of *Four Flowers* (Luc's latest poem), on a middle page written in red pencil: I LOVE YOU in very large letters, in her hand, by her, and a lock of her hair in the fold. Luc Pascal arrived in Paris with the copy of *Four Flowers* against his breast, and because those fateful letters were written, the insuperable unhappiness had not yet arrived, he was able to live; he opened the book in the streets and reread the letters.

He reentered his dark apartment on the Left Bank, on the mezzanine floor with houses opposite, the way one puts back on a dead skin. What he was losing of himself in a single instant was incalculable. But patience; he was here for only a few days, for an hour. When he opened the windows after two years, a rain of soot, cobwebs, and all the leprosy of things fell softly on his head. He seized a broom and cleaned the horrible little box of a human life in Paris, in the midst of a scummy boulevard noise, amid the stairway clatter and the concierge smells, and the obstinate invective "shit, shit" rising from the street.

He was not present here. But he asked the Fire of Heaven to reduce to ashes the base apparitions that surrounded him. He closed his eyes for a long time: Baladine alive. Baladine rosy and ripening on a large patch of blue (probably the lake), with small, sugary clouds above her. Baladine smokes her Abdullah, crossing her legs. Baladine preoccupied, attentive, has an idea. Baladine naked, crouching. Baladine in the midst of the sky. Baladine talks numbers. Baladine washes herself in a ray of sunlight in winter. Baladine crosses the bedroom without clothes. Baladine powdered. Baladine looks at you from below. Baladine claps her hands. Baladine comes back at twenty past noon and throws her hat on the bed. Baladine listens to a poem. She kisses Pierrot. She argues with passion and gentleness. Baladine walks on the Conches road in the morning like a gazelle. Baladine, the evening of the crickets, at last takes off her dress. Baladine at Lucerne is a wonderful, slightly plump back that one strokes with one's hand. Baladine, Baladine, Baladine.

Could she be dead, then? No, a sign is enough. The sign will occur, she is already coming back. He was not even in a hurry to look for her, so sure was he of recapturing her entirely.

Then he plunged outside: where should he go?

XLIX

Life, real affecting life, life, life is there, I have only to reach out my hand—I have it, snap, a misfortune—layer of ice forms—I don't have it anymore, too late.

He had begun his search.

First days, first weeks, first months. He went to all the places where she could be, of which they had sometimes talked: he went into the tea houses, the department stores; he examined the boulevard from the Café de la Paix, he entered music halls; he telephoned all the middle-class hotels, then he poked around in the poor hotels of the Left Bank; he had begun with the Luxembourg and Montparnasse, but this was as immense as the sea. To do this he needed a monstrous energy. He asked everywhere, he described (in vain) a Madame Pascal, or a Madame Sergounine, with a young child, his clothes like these, brown or blue. Because he could have died of sorrow over always saying the same thing, he had an infernal tenacity, and at police headquarters they looked at him curiously. On his wife's trail he put M. Louis Joseph, ex-inspector of the Sûreté, private policeman in the foremost company in the world: "confidential information, infidelity, health, morality, research into missing persons in the interest of the families," etc., etc.

An idiot with a mustache turned up every week and gave him his report: absurd stories.

Oh Baladine, oh Baladine, oh genital rose!

At the same time he closed his soul entirely in all directions that led toward the outside. If he was searching for Baladine, it was in the depths of himself.

He felt no resentment toward her. He never asked the question: why did she leave? He preferred to remember.

It was in this way that he found himself with her at Morges, where they had spent a month during the preceding summer: one must imagine a great big old house standing by itself in front of reeds, and two people in love. In this spot the reeds form a moving and always balanced border between the water of the lake and the earth of the fields and the roads along which tall poplars grow. His gaze joined to hers followed the swallows: she loved them so much! In the middle of the dilapidated room

117

with its five windows he was composing *The Dry Earth*, a novel; dictated the text of the first draft to Baladine—there he is and there she is—she is sitting at the typewriter—he walks to and fro—looks at her back, the nape of her neck, her active hands with their rings—hears the noise—sees Baladine's bent thigh, important and silent—and by means of all this he sinks gradually, fiercely, and always more and more into himself; there he finds sweetness as regards himself, and there discovers his characters. The country open on all sides, too vast, responds with its silence. Isolation is what genius deserves. *She* is beautiful. Let division and dissolution continue elsewhere; the destiny of Luc Pascal is a closed house containing within it Heaven . . . Alas, alas, genital rose!

L

Because he had tortured it so, Baladine's Face sat down on a sofa and looked at him. Baladine's Face (it was Baladine). (The immemorial echo of Baladine's presence was produced, the face was cold, stately, sweet, a little tipped back; the vague body formed an extension, magnificent and without importance. Dressed? Not dressed? As you like.)

Yes, she sat down on the sofa in the dark apartment and began by being silent for a long time, natural, with a striking immobility in her gaze, certain small and incomprehensible gestures with her fingertips, and Luc looked at her courageously in such a way that a day passed between them passed like the blink of the eye.

At first, Luc had to make a certain effort to obtain her. He also had to give up all work for some time before evoking her. She was more spontaneous at night, more incomplete and disturbing in the day. Why would Luc have spoken to her? One doesn't speak to an image. However, once she gave herself to him in bed, during the insomnia he so often had before dawn. Certainly she had chosen the moment when all of creation became confused in Luc's brain. Besides, "she gave herself" is a manner of speaking. Since she was only a Face.

When she came to him, Luc assumed the position she liked best, his elbow resting on the table and his hand supporting his forehead. "Because she always said that she dearly loved my hand." Baladine Face was always in the same corner, the one the brightness from the window hardly touched—knowing that against the background her pale face stood out perfectly and was alive. The lips moved, and Luc understood that Baladine was talking to herself; she was quite right. The lips were made up and were the last thing to disappear when the image went away.

Luc Pascal soon arranged his whole life around her.

LI

He grew used to it. Obviously he was still looking for the real Baladine in the city, obeying a conventional impulse, and more than anything else through his own impetus. Baladine Face was beginning to make him understand some things. For instance, that this police business had gone on long enough; he fired everyone.

When he went out, he would follow a woman, for example. He had not had the idea of it at first but suddenly gave way. What? He saw only her back, her high heels, her swaying hips, her slightly gray hair cut short—her! Baladine Face had disappeared, and even Luc Pascal . . . He rushes toward the woman and touches her. A stranger turns around. Luc stammers a speech of apology. Baladine Face would return later and laugh.

He played this game for a short while and then stopped it. He had wanted to confront true and false reality.

He wanted to go further, and in order to show that Baladine Face was surpassing everyone, he found the means to thrust himself (disguised as a Mongol) on a movie actress. But this woman demanded violence, brutality, insult. More worthy was the mysterious image that deserved these things more.

He did not associate with a single man with whom one could have a conversation. He was in contact with the concierge, the cleaning woman, the milkman, and the laundress. He locked himself in with a double lock. Everything he had to do he dealt with by letter, and the answer came to him under the door. He had aged in a curious way: a multitude of delicate wrinkles around his mouth and his lusterless eyes. He suffered from long headaches and swallowed aspirin. He returned to working a considerable amount, wrote by day, reread (and tore up) at night. He thought a good deal about the cross at Brigue. There were anniversaries of that cross. On those days, Baladine Face was very gentle to Luc.

For the rest, the Face was now more loving; watching over the work and over the man. She stayed to encircle him in this way: standing behind him as he sat, enclosing his head with a bare arm; while she was above, always cold, always Baladine, always leaning back.

When she made him a prisoner, he had the means to reflect infinitely and to find himself thoroughly in the heart of things.

LII

"But don't you understand that in Morges, my dear, you were a swine and a monster, that was my last word on the subject. Go on, I knew you, weren't you poisoning me with your selfishness, and your sacred body—will you deny it?—didn't you use me as a whore at night and a secretary during the day, on the sofa when he wants it, at the typewriter when he desires it, and the nasty things you did, you have forgotten them. 'Your back is preventing me from thinking, go change your dress'—I who had made a life for myself and who had known a few men! At Lucerne you were more of a p—, but nicer."

After a horrible succession of trivialities, Baladine's Face went on quite differently.

"As she was henceforth replacing the real thing for him, and as it was understood that nothing would bring Baladine back or reestablish his love for her merely in order to make the past intelligible to him and explain the inevitable, she reproached him for having played, during the last six months of their life in Switzerland, *a role* whose diabolical character was unquestionable; for having undertaken an experiment by erecting separations, partitions, and walls between everything that was he and everything that was he and Baladine; for having shown *cruelties* and crudenesses that were, so to speak, gratuitous, useless; for having made himself worse than he was in relation to her; for having in fact deliberately created a character who *enjoyed* destroying the feelings around him. She had supported, supported, and supported him with patience until the middle of winter, convinced that this was a role (and even, at the last minute, she had trusted in *marriage*), convinced that the *superior* man who had twice caused himself to be loved and twice seduced her but had engaged in the wonderful discourse about Jacques could not have changed so much in the course of a summer that he would trample on what Jacques had properly left in her of purity and sweetness, and what he himself, Luc Pascal, claimed to want to make in full accord with the memory of Jacques."

Luc answered the Face of Baladine: "I don't think I lied, or acted reprehensibly. I did not understand that she would leave the day after the marriage."

Baladine's Face, then: "What you had the will to create with Jacques, you no longer thought anything about. So you wanted to subject your love for both of them to a sort of humiliation. You betrayed your vow to love her by finding Jacques again in her heart, as there was nothing real left there, as it was without goodness. And furthermore, what violence did you do her child the day you told him that his father had killed himself?"

LIII

Baladine's Face then detached itself from all these things, and its face became pure again. It left Baladine and the past alone, it was only a spirit.

He is sitting down. Or perhaps he is standing. Opposites join, such as: day-night, silence-din, dream-waking, presence-nonpresence. He is sitting in his dark apartment at the hour of noon, and his appearance is that of a person in ill health whose gaze is inhabited by an active flame that is green and spiritual.

His body is almost always in the same position, and the progress of his thoughts is not exteriorized by any motion: nothing is discernable. An absolute hardness, almost inhuman, is created. The hardness encloses the disharmony, he is in disharmony with everything. Fine weather commits him to melancholy, and love with a woman is impossible as soon as she is truly willing. The slightest event is an iron barrier raised against him. He beats a retreat with sweat on his forehead. The fracture is first of all profoundly in himself (he says that his heart is dying), but one cannot be sure this is painful; here he is, far from what he has to understand, from what he would have to do, from what he could be.

As he has no direct relations with any so-called intellectual person, and as his overly essential books cannot find a favorable reception because they arouse no pleasure, he will see his work, the last living part of his soul and the thing for which he was put on earth, sink gradually before his eyes into the region of oblivion.

This is why his muteness contains interminable contradictory exchanges and his immobility fits of agitation. More than ever he lives with those who love him: the Face of Baladine, and also the Other—Jacques. From the mouth of the Face thought can emerge, poetry. The Other waits for him outdoors, on the sidewalk; slipping an arm through his arm, it falls into step and accompanies him.

He rarely writes, even though there is a great deal of paper in front of him; if one word is crossed out on a page, he throws the sheet away and begins again. He cannot read any literature; he cannot tolerate the sight of books; he becomes exceptionally ignorant.

What does he look at in front of him? Things, houses, the inanimate, the sky. How does he live? Sometimes he can work. How does money come to him? He has no idea. He must wait. Is he getting ready to die? Probably.

Luc Pascal is still alive, he exists only in that second in which Poetry enters him and speaks; and, because he knows that it is eternal life, he would like to hold onto it always; he is lightened, happy, only in the moment when, after having waited miserably for a long time, he is suddenly recompensed by the awareness of being in the infinite place, the only state of mind necessary. In flashes Luc Pascal revives; he is one, he shouts for joy; his youth is so young it would startle any adolescent. But the brief ray dies, the phantoms reappear; this is Luc's nonexistence.

LIV

A blue flower on the mountain.

The End